SHORT STORIES

IVAN S. TURGENEV

SANAGE
PUBLISHING HOUSE

Paperback: 978-936205642-9
Hardback: 978-936205030-4
eBook: 978-936205511-8

Any references to historical events, real people, or real places are used fictitiously. Names, characters, and places are products of the author's imagination.

Printed by: Manipal Technologies Limited, India

Sanage Publishing House LLP
Mumbai, India

sanagepublishing@gmail.com

Ivan Sergeyevich Turgenev was a Russian novelist, short story writer, poet, playwright, translator and popularizer of Russian literature in the West.

His first major publication, a short story collection titled A Sportsman's Sketches (1852), was a milestone of Russian realism. His novel Fathers and Sons (1862) is regarded as one of the major works of 19th-century fiction.

Contents

AN UNHAPPY GIRL

Yes, yes, Piotr Gavrilovitch began; those were painful days... and I would rather not recall them.... But I have made you a promise; I shall have to tell you the whole story. Listen.

I

I was living at that time (the winter of 1835) in Moscow, in the house of my aunt, the sister of my dead mother. I was eighteen; I had only just passed from the second into the third course in the faculty 'of Language' (that was what it was called in those days) in the Moscow University. My aunt was a gentle, quiet woman—a widow. She lived in a big, wooden house in Ostozhonka, one of those warm, cosy houses such as, I fancy, one can find nowhere else but in Moscow. She saw hardly anyone, sat from morning till night in the drawing-room with two companions, drank the choicest tea, played patience, and was continually requesting that the room be fumigated. Thereupon her companions ran into the hall; a few minutes later an old servant in livery would bring in a copper pan with a bunch of mint on a hot brick, and stepping hurriedly upon the narrow strips of carpet, he would sprinkle the mint with vinegar. White fumes always puffed up about his wrinkled face, and he frowned and turned away, while the canaries in the dining-room chirped their hardest, exasperated by the hissing of the smouldering mint.

I was fatherless and motherless, and my aunt spoiled me. She placed the whole of the ground floor at my complete disposal. My rooms were furnished very elegantly, not at all like a student's rooms in fact: there were pink curtains in the bedroom, and a muslin canopy, adorned with blue rosettes, towered over my bed. Those rosettes were, I'll own, rather an annoyance to me; to my thinking, such 'effeminacies' were calculated to lower me in the eyes of my companions. As it was, they nicknamed me 'the boarding-school miss.' I could never succeed in forcing myself to smoke. I studied—why conceal my shortcomings?—very lazily, especially at the beginning of the course. I went out a great deal. My aunt had bestowed on me a wide sledge, fit for a general, with a pair of sleek horses. At the houses of 'the gentry' my visits were rare, but at the theatre I was quite at home, and I consumed masses of tarts at the restaurants. For all that, I permitted myself no breach of decorum, and behaved very discreetly, *en jeune homme de bonne maison*. I would not for anything in the world have pained my kind aunt; and besides I was naturally of a rather cool temperament.

II

From my earliest years I had been fond of chess; I had no idea of the science of the game, but I didn't play badly. One day in a café, I was the spectator of a prolonged contest at chess, between two players, of whom one, a fair-haired young man of about five-and-twenty, struck me as playing well. The game ended in his favour; I offered to play a match with him. He agreed,... and in the course of an hour, beat me easily, three times running.

'You have a natural gift for the game,' he pronounced in a courteous tone, noticing probably that my vanity was suffering; 'but you don't know the openings. You ought to study a chess-book—Allgacir or Petrov.'

'Do you think so? But where can I get such a book?'

'Come to me; I will give you one.'

He gave me his name and told me where he was living. Next day I went to see him, and a week later we were almost inseparable.

III

My new acquaintance was called Alexander Davidovitch Fustov. He lived with his mother, a rather wealthy woman, the widow of a privy councillor but he occupied a little lodge apart and lived quite independently, just as I did at my aunt's. He had a post in the department of Court affairs. I became genuinely attached to him. I had never in my life met a young man more 'sympathetic.' Everything about him was charming and attractive: his graceful figure, his bearing, his voice, and especially his small, delicate face with the golden-blue eyes, the elegant, as it were coquettishly moulded little nose, the unchanging amiable smile on the crimson lips, the light curls of soft hair over the rather narrow, snow-white brow. Fustov's character was remarkable for exceptional serenity, and a sort of amiable, restrained affability; he was never pre-occupied, and was always satisfied with everything; but on the other hand, he was never ecstatic over anything. Every excess, even in a good feeling, jarred upon him; 'that's savage, savage,' he would say with a faint shrug, half closing his golden eyes. Marvellous were those eyes of Fustov's! They invariably expressed sympathy, good-will, even devotion. It was only at a later period that I noticed that the expression of his eyes resulted solely from their setting, that it never changed, even when he was sipping his soup or smoking a cigar. His preciseness became a byword between us. His grandmother, indeed, had been a German. Nature had endowed him with all sorts of talents. He danced capitally, was a dashing horseman, and a first-rate swimmer; did carpentering, carving and joinery, bound books and cut out silhouettes, painted in watercolours nosegays of flowers or Napoleon in profile in a blue uniform; played the zither with feeling; knew a number of tricks, with cards and without; and had a fair knowledge of mechanics, physics and chemistry; but everything only up to a certain point. Only for languages he had no great facility: even French he spoke rather badly. He spoke in general little, and his share in our students' discussions was mostly limited to the bright sympathy of his glance and smile. To the fair sex Fustov was attractive, undoubtedly, but on this subject, of such importance among young people, he did not care to enlarge, and fully deserved the nickname given him by his comrades, 'the discreet Don Juan.' I was not dazzled by Fustov; there was nothing in him to dazzle, but I prized his affection, though in reality it was only manifested by his never refusing to see me when I called. To my mind Fustov was the happiest man in the world. His life ran so very smoothly. His mother, brothers, sisters, aunts, and uncles all adored him, he was on exceptionally good terms with all of them and enjoyed the reputation of a paragon in his family.

IV

One day I went round to him rather early and did not find him in his study. He called to me from the next room; sounds of panting and splashing reached me from there. Every morning Fustov took a cold shower-bath and afterwards for a quarter of an hour practised gymnastic exercises, in which he had attained remarkable proficiency. Excessive anxiety about one's physical health he did not approve of, but he did not neglect necessary care. ('Don't neglect yourself, don't over-excite yourself, work in moderation,' was his precept.) Fustov had not yet made his appearance, when the outer door of the room where I was waiting flew wide open, and there walked in a man about fifty, wearing a bluish uniform. He was a stout, squarely-built man with milky-whitish eyes in a dark-red face and a perfect cap of thick, grey, curly hair. This person stopped short, looked at me, opened his mouth wide, and with a metallic chuckle, he gave himself a smart slap on his haunch, kicking his leg up in front as he did so.

'Ivan Demianitch?' my friend inquired through the door.

'The same, at your service,' the newcomer responded. 'What are you up to? At your toilette? That's right! that's right!' (The voice of the man addressed as Ivan Demianitch had the same harsh, metallic note as his laugh.) 'I've trudged all this way to give your little brother his lesson; and he's got a cold, you know, and does nothing but sneeze. He can't do his work. So, I've looked in on you for a bit to warm myself.'

Ivan Demianitch laughed again the same strange guffaw, again dealt himself a sounding smack on the leg, and pulling a check handkerchief out of his pocket, blew his nose noisily, ferociously rolling his eyes, spat into the handkerchief, and ejaculated with the whole force of his lungs: 'Tfoo-o-o!'

Fustov came into the room, and shaking hands with both of us, asked us if we were acquainted.

'Not a bit of it!' Ivan Demianitch boomed at once: 'the veteran of the year twelve has not that honour!'

Fustov mentioned my name first, then, indicating the 'veteran of the year twelve,' he pronounced: 'Ivan Demianitch Ratsch, professor of... various subjects.'

'Precisely so, various they are, precisely,' Mr. Ratsch chimed in. 'Come to think of it, what is there I haven't taught, and that I'm not teaching now, for that matter! Mathematics and geography and statistics and Italian book-keeping, ha-ha ha-ha! and music! You doubt it, my dear sir?'—he pounced suddenly upon me—'ask Alexander Daviditch if I'm not first-rate on the bassoon. I should be a poor sort of Bohemian—Czech, I should say—if I weren't! Yes, sir, I'm a Czech, and my native place is ancient Prague! By the way, Alexander Daviditch, why haven't we seen you for so long! We ought to have a little duet... ha-ha! Really!'

'I was at your place the day before yesterday, Ivan Demianitch,' replied Fustov.

'But I call that a long while, ha-ha!'

When Mr. Ratsch laughed, his white eyes shifted from side to side in a strange, restless way.

'You're surprised, young man, I see, at my behaviour,' he addressed me again. 'But that's because you don't understand my temperament. You must just ask our good friend here, Alexander Daviditch, to tell you about me. What'll he tell you? He'll tell you old Ratsch is a simple, good-hearted chap, a regular Russian, in heart, if not in origin, ha-ha! At his christening named Johann Dietrich, but always called Ivan Demianitch! What's in my mind pops out on my tongue; I wear my heart, as they say, on my sleeve. Ceremony of all sorts I know naught about and don't want to either! Can't bear it! You drop in on me one day of an evening, and you'll see for yourself. My good woman—my wife, that is—has no nonsense about her either; she'll cook and bake you... something wonderful! Alexander Daviditch, isn't it the truth I'm telling?'

Fustov only smiled, and I remained silent.

'Don't look down on the old fellow, but come round,' pursued Mr. Ratsch. 'But now...' (he pulled a fat silver watch out of his pocket and put it up to one of his goggle eyes)'I'd better be toddling on, I suppose. I've another chick expecting me.... Devil knows what I'm teaching him,... mythology, by God! And he lives a long way off, the rascal, at the Red Gate! No matter: I'll toddle off on foot. Thanks to your brother's cutting his lesson, I shall be the fifteen kopecks for sledge hire to the good! Ha-ha! A very good day to you, gentlemen, till we meet again!... Eh?... We must have a little duet!' Mr. Ratsch bawled from the passage putting on his goloshes noisily, and for the last time we heard his metallic laugh.

V

'What a strange man!' I said, turning to Fustov, who had already set to work at his turning-lathe. 'Can he be a foreigner? He speaks Russian so fluently.'

'He is a foreigner; only he's been thirty years in Russia. As long ago as 1802, some prince or other brought him from abroad... in the capacity of secretary... more likely, valet, one would suppose. He does speak Russian fluently, certainly.'

'With such go, such far-fetched turns and phrases,' I put in.

'Well, yes. Only very unnaturally too. They're all like that, these Russianised Germans.'

'But he's a Czech, isn't he?'

'I don't know; maybe. He talks German with his wife.'

'And why does he call himself a veteran of the year twelve? Was he in the militia, or what?'

'In the militia! indeed! At the time of the fire, he remained in Moscow and lost all his property.... That was all he did.'

'But what did he stay in Moscow for?'

Fustov still went on with his turning.

'The Lord knows. I have heard that he was a spy on our side; but that must be nonsense. But it's a fact that he received compensation from the treasury for his losses.'

'He wears some sort of uniform.... I suppose he's in government service then?'

'Yes. Professor in the cadet's corps. He has the rank of a petty councillor.'

'What's his wife like?'

'A German settled here, daughter of a sausage maker... or butcher....'

'And do you often go to see him?'

'Yes.'

'What, is it pleasant there?'

'Rather pleasant.'

'Has he have any children?'

'Yes. Three by the German, and a son and daughter by his first wife.'

'And how old is the eldest daughter?'

'About five-and-twenty,'

I fancied Fustov bent lower over his lathe, and the wheel turned more rapidly, and hummed under the even strokes of his feet.

'Is she good-looking?'

'That's a matter of taste. She has a remarkable face, and she's altogether... a remarkable person.'

'Aha!' thought I. Fustov continued his work with special earnestness, and to my next question he only responded by a grunt.

'I must make her acquaintance,' I decided.

VI

A few days later, Fustov and I set off to Mr. Ratsch's to spend the evening. He lived in a wooden house with a big yard and garden, in Krivoy Place near the Pretchistensky boulevard. He came out into the passage and meeting us with his characteristic jarring guffaw and noise, led us at once into the drawing-room, where he presented me to a stout lady in a skimpy canvas gown, Eleonora Karpovna, his wife. Eleonora Karpovna had most likely in her first youth been possessed of what the French for some unknown reason call *beauté du diable*, that is to say, freshness; but when I made her acquaintance, she suggested involuntarily to the mind a good-sized piece of meat, freshly laid by the butcher on a clean marble table. Designedly I used the word 'clean'; not only our hostess herself seemed a model of cleanliness, but everything about her, everything in the house positively shone, and glittered; everything had been scoured, and polished, and washed: the samovar on the round table flashed like fire; the curtains before the windows, the table-napkins were crisp with starch, as were also the little frocks and shirts of Mr. Ratsch's four children sitting there, stout, chubby little creatures, exceedingly like their mother, with coarsely moulded, sturdy faces, curls on their foreheads, and red, shapeless fingers. All four of them had rather flat noses, large, swollen-looking lips, and tiny, light-grey eyes.

'Here's my squadron!' cried Mr. Ratsch, laying his heavy hand on the children's heads one after another. 'Kolia, Olga, Sashka and Mashka! This one's eight, this one's seven, that one's four, and this one's only two! Ha! ha! ha! As you can see, my wife and I haven't wasted our time! Eh, Eleonora Karpovna?'

'You always say things like that,' observed Eleonora Karpovna and she turned away.

'And she's bestowed such Russian names on her squallers!' Mr. Ratsch pursued. 'The next thing, she'll have them all baptized into the Orthodox Church! Yes, by Jove! She's so Slavonic in her sympathies, 'pon my soul, she is, though she is of German blood! Eleonora Karpovna, are you Slavonic?'

Eleonora Karpovna lost her temper.

'I'm a petty councillor's wife, that's what I am! And so, I'm a Russian lady and all you may say....'

'There, the way she loves Russia, it's simply awful!' broke in Ivan Demianitch. 'A perfect volcano, ho, ho!'

'Well, and what of it?' pursued Eleonora Karpovna. 'To be sure I love Russia, for where else could I obtain noble rank? And my children too are nobly born, you know. Kolia, sitze ruhig mit den Füssen!'

Ratsch waved his hand to her.

'There, there, princess, don't excite yourself! But where's the nobly born Viktor? To be sure, he's always gadding about! He'll come across the inspector one of these fine days! He'll give him a talking-to! Das ist ein Bummler, Fiktor!'

'Dem Fiktov kann ich nicht kommandiren, Ivan Demianitch. Sie wissen wohl!' grumbled Eleonora Karpovna.

I looked at Fustov, as though wishing finally to arrive at what induced him to visit such people... but at that instant there came into the room a tall girl in a black dress, the elder daughter of Mr. Ratsch, to whom Fustov had referred.... I perceived the explanation of my friend's frequent visits.

VII

There is somewhere, I remember, in Shakespeare, something about 'a white dove in a flock of black crows'; that was just the impression made on me by the girl, who entered the room. Between the world surrounding her and herself there seemed to be too little in common; she herself seemed secretly bewildered and wondering how she had come there. All the members of Mr. Ratsch's family looked self-satisfied, simple-hearted, healthy creatures; her beautiful, but already careworn, face bore the traces of depression, pride and morbidity. The others, unmistakable plebeians, were unconstrained in their manners, coarse perhaps, but simple; but a painful uneasiness was manifest in all her indubitably aristocratic nature. In her very exterior there was no trace of the type characteristic of the German race; she recalled rather the children of the south. The excessively thick, lustreless black hair, the hollow, black, lifeless but beautiful eyes, the low, prominent brow, the aquiline nose, the livid pallor of the smooth skin, a certain tragic line near the delicate lips, and in the slightly sunken cheeks, something abrupt, and at the same time helpless in the movements, elegance without gracefulness... in Italy all this would not have struck me as exceptional, but in Moscow, near the Pretchistensky boulevard, it simply astonished me! I got up from my seat on her entrance; she flung me a swift, uneasy glance, and dropping her black eyelashes, sat down near the window 'like Tatiana.' (Pushkin's *Oniegin* was then fresh in every one's mind.) I glanced at Fustov, but my friend was standing with his back to me, taking a cup of tea from the plump hands of Eleonora Karpovna. I noticed further that the girl as she came in seemed to bring with her a breath of slight physical chillness.... 'What a statue!' was my thought.

VIII

'Piotr Gavrilitch,' thundered Mr. Ratsch, turning to me, 'let me introduce you to my... to my... my number one, ha, ha, ha! to Susanna Ivanovna!'

I bowed in silence, and thought at once: 'Why, the name too is not the same sort as the others,' while Susanna rose slightly, without smiling or loosening her tightly clasped hands.

'And how about the duet?' Ivan Demianitch pursued: 'Alexander Daviditch? eh? benefactor! Your zither was left with us, and I've got the bassoon out of its case already. Let us make sweet music for the honourable company!' (Mr. Ratsch liked to display his Russian; he was continually bursting out with expressions, such as those which are strewn broadcast about the ultra-national poems of Prince Viazemsky.) 'What do you say? Carried?' cried Ivan Demianitch, seeing Fustov made no objection. 'Kolka, march into the study, and look sharp with the music-stand! Olga, this way with the zither! And oblige us with candles for the stands, better-half!' (Mr. Ratsch turned round and round in the room like a top.) 'Piotr Gavrilitch, you like music, hey? If you don't care for it, you must amuse yourself with conversation, only mind, not above a whisper! Ha, ha ha! But whatever's become of that silly chap, Viktor? He ought to be here to listen too! You spoil him completely, Eleonora Karpovna.'

Eleonora Karpovna fired up angrily.

'Aber was kann ich denn, Ivan Demianitch...'

'All right, all right, don't squabble! Bleibe ruhig, hast verstanden? Alexander Daviditch! at your service, sir!'

The children had promptly done as their father had told them. The music-stands were set up, the music began. I have already mentioned that Fustov played the zither extremely well, but that instrument has always produced the most distressing impression upon me. I have always fancied, and I fancy still, that there is imprisoned in the zither the soul of a decrepit Jew money-lender, and that it emits nasal whines and complaints against the merciless musician who forces it to utter sounds. Mr. Ratsch's performance, too, was not calculated to give me much pleasure; moreover, his face became suddenly purple, and assumed a malignant expression, while his whitish eyes rolled viciously, as though he were just about to murder someone with his bassoon, and were swearing and threatening by way of preliminary, puffing out chokingly husky, coarse notes one after another. I placed myself near Susanna, and waiting for a momentary pause, I asked her if she were as fond of music as her papa.

She turned away, as though I had given her a shove, and pronounced abruptly, 'Who?'

'Your father,' I repeated,' Mr. Ratsch.'

'Mr. Ratsch is not my father.'

'Not your father! I beg your pardon... I must have misunderstood... But I remember, Alexander Daviditch...'

Susanna looked at me intently and shyly.

'You misunderstood Mr. Fustov. Mr. Ratsch is my stepfather.'

I was silent for a while.

'And you don't care for music?' I began again.

Susanna glanced at me again. Undoubtedly there was something suggesting a wild creature in her eyes. She obviously had not expected nor desired the continuation of our conversation.

'I did not say that' she brought out slowly. 'Troo-too-too-too-too-oo-oo...' the bassoon growled with startling fury, executing the final flourishes. I turned round, caught sight of the red neck of Mr. Ratsch, swollen like a boa-constrictor's, beneath his projecting ears, and very disgusting I thought him.

'But that... instrument you surely do not care for,' I said in an undertone.

'No... I don't care for it,' she responded, as though catching my secret hint.

'Oho!' thought I, and felt, as it were, delighted at something.

'Susanna Ivanovna,' Eleonora Karpovna announced suddenly in her German Russian, 'music greatly loves, and herself very beautifully plays the piano, only she likes not to play the piano when she is greatly pressed to play.'

Susanna made Eleonora Karpovna no reply—she did not even look at her—only there was a faint movement of her eyes, under their dropped lids, in her direction. From this movement alone—this movement of her pupils—I could perceive what was the nature of the feeling Susanna cherished for the second wife of her stepfather.... And again, I was delighted at something.

Meanwhile the duet was over. Fustov got up and with hesitating footsteps approached the window, near which Susanna and I were sitting, and asked her if she had received from Lengold's the music that he had promised to order her from Petersburg.

'Selections from *Robert le Diable,*' he added, turning to me, 'from that new opera that every one's making such a fuss about.'

'No, I haven't got it yet,' answered Susanna, and turning round with her face to the window she whispered hurriedly. 'Please, Alexander Daviditch, I entreat you, don't make me play today. I don't feel in the mood a bit.'

'What's that? Robert le Diable of Meyer-beer?' bellowed Ivan Demianitch, coming up to us: 'I don't mind betting it's a first-class article! He's a Jew, and all Jews, like all Czechs, are born musicians. Especially Jews. That's right, isn't it, Susanna Ivanovna? Hey? Ha, ha, ha, ha!'

In Mr. Ratsch's last words, and this time even in his guffaw, there could be heard something more than his usual bantering tone—the desire to wound was evident. So, at least, I fancied, and so Susanna understood him. She started instinctively, flushed red, and bit her lower lip. A spot of light, like the gleam of a tear, flashed on her eyelash, and rising quickly, she went out of the room.

'Where are you off to, Susanna Ivanovna?' Mr. Ratsch bawled after her.

'Let her be, Ivan Demianitch, 'put in Eleonora Karpovna. 'Wenn sie einmal so et was im Kopfe hat...'

'A nervous temperament,' Ratsch pronounced, rotating on his heels, and slapping himself on the haunch, 'suffers with the *plexus solaris.* Oh! you needn't look at me like that, Piotr Gavrilitch! I've had a go at anatomy too, ha, ha! I'm even a bit of a doctor! You ask Eleonora Karpovna... I cure all her little ailments! Oh, I'm a famous hand at that!'

'You must forever be joking, Ivan Demianitch,' the latter responded with displeasure, while Fustov, laughing and gracefully swaying to and fro, looked at the husband and wife.

'And why not be joking, mein Mütterchen?' retorted Ivan Demianitch. 'Life's given us for use, and still more for beauty, as some celebrated poet has observed. Kolka, wipe your nose, little savage!'

IX

'I was put in a very awkward position this evening through your doing,' I said the same evening to Fustov, on the way home with him. 'You told me that that girl—what's her name?—Susanna, was the daughter of Mr. Ratsch, but she's his stepdaughter.'

'Really! Did I tell you she was his daughter? But... isn't it all the same?'

'That Ratsch,' I went on.... 'O Alexander, how I detest him! Did you notice the peculiar sneer with which he spoke of Jews before her? Is she... a Jewess?'

Fustov walked ahead, swinging his arms; it was cold, the snow was crisp, like salt, under our feet.

'Yes, I recollect, I did hear something of the sort,' he observed at last.... 'Her mother, I fancy, was of Jewish extraction.'

'Then must Mr. Ratsch have married a widow the first time?'

'Probably.'

'H'm!... And that Viktor, who didn't come in this evening, is his stepson too?'

'No... he's his real son. But, as you know, I don't enter into other people's affairs, and I don't like asking questions. I'm not inquisitive.'

I bit my tongue. Fustov still pushed on ahead. As we got near home, I overtook him and peeped into his face.

'Oh!' I queried, 'is Susanna really so musical?'

Fustov frowned.

'She plays the piano well, 'he said between his teeth. 'Only she's very shy, I warn you!' he added with a slight grimace. He seemed to be regretting having made me acquainted with her.

I said nothing and we parted.

X

Next morning I set off again to Fustov's. To spend my mornings at his rooms had become a necessity for me. He received me cordially, as usual, but of our visit of the previous evening—not a word! As though he had taken water into his mouth, as they say. I began turning over the pages of the last number of the *Telescope.*

A person, unknown to me, came into the room. It turned out to be Mr. Ratsch's son, the Viktor whose absence had been censured by his father the evening before.

He was a young man, about eighteen, but already looked dissipated and unhealthy, with a mawkishly insolent grin on his unclean face, and an expression of fatigue in his swollen eyes. He was like his father, only his features were smaller and not without a certain prettiness. But in this very prettiness there was something offensive. He was dressed in a very slovenly way; there were buttons off his undergraduate's coat, one of his boots had a hole in it, and he fairly reeked of tobacco.

'How d'ye do,' he said in a sleepy voice, with those peculiar twitching's of the head and shoulders which I have always noticed in spoilt and conceited young men. 'I meant to go to the University, but here I am. Sort of oppression on my chest. Give us a cigar.' He walked right across the room, listlessly dragging his feet, and keeping his hands in his trouser-pockets, and sank heavily upon the sofa.

'Have you caught cold?' asked Fustov, and he introduced us to each other. We were both students but were in different faculties.

'No!... Likely! Yesterday, I must own...' (here Ratsch junior smiled, again not without a certain prettiness, though he showed a set of bad teeth) 'I was drunk, awfully drunk. Yes'—he lighted a cigar and cleared his throat—'Obihodov's farewell supper.'

'Where's he going?'

'To the Caucasus and taking his young lady with him. You know the black-eyed girl, with the freckles. Silly fool!'

'Your father was asking after you yesterday,' observed Fustov.

Viktor spat aside. 'Yes, I heard about it. You were at our den yesterday. Well, music, eh?'

'As usual.'

'And *she*... with a new visitor' (here he pointed with his head in my direction) 'she gave herself airs; I'll be bound. Wouldn't it play, eh?'

'Of whom are you speaking?' Fustov asked.

'Why, of the most honoured Susanna Ivanovna, of course!'

Viktor lolled still more comfortably, put his arm up round his head, gazed at his own hand, and cleared his throat hoarsely.

I glanced at Fustov. He merely shrugged his shoulders, as though giving me to understand that it was no use talking to such a dolt.

XI

Viktor, staring at the ceiling, fell to talking, deliberately and through his nose, of the theatre, of two actors he knew, of a certain Serafrina Serafrinovna, who had 'made a fool' of him, of the new professor, R., whom he called a brute. 'Because, only fancy, what a monstrous notion! Every lecture he begins with calling over the students' names, and he's reckoned a liberal too! I'd have all your liberals locked up in custody!' and turning at last his full face and whole body towards Fustov, he brought out in a half-plaintive, half-ironical voice: 'I wanted to ask you something, Alexander Daviditch.... Couldn't you talk my governor round somehow?... You play duets with him, you know.... Here he gives me five miserable blue notes a month.... What's the use of that! Not enough for tobacco. And then he goes on about my not making debts! I should like to put him in my place, and then we should see! I don't come in for pensions, not like *some people*.' (Viktor pronounced these last words with peculiar emphasis.) 'But he's got a lot of tin, I know! It's no use his whining about hard times, there's no taking me in. No fear! He's made a snug little pile!'

Fustov looked dubiously at Victor.

'If you like,' he began, 'I'll speak to your father. Or, if you like... meanwhile... a trifling sum....'

'Oh, no! Better get round the governor... Though,' added Viktor, scratching his nose with all his fingers at once, 'you might hand over five-and-twenty roubles, if it's the same to you.... What's the blessed total I owe you?'

'You've borrowed eighty-five roubles of me.'

'Yes.... Well, that's all right, then... make it a hundred and ten. I'll pay it all in a lump.'

Fustov went into the next room, brought back a twenty-five-rouble note and handed it in silence to Viktor. The latter took it, yawned with his mouth wide open, grumbled thanks, and, shrugging and stretching, got up from the sofa.

'Foo! though... I'm bored,' he muttered, 'might as well turn in to the "Italie."'

He moved towards the door.

Fustov looked after him. He seemed to be struggling with himself.

'What pension were you alluding to just now, Viktor Ivanitch?' he asked at last.

Viktor stopped in the doorway and put on his cap.

'Oh, don't you know? Susanna Ivanovna's pension.... She gets one. An awfully curious story, I can tell you! I'll tell you one of these days. Quite an affair, 'pon my soul, a queer affair. But, I say, the governor, you won't forget about the governor, please! His hide is thick, of course—German, and it's had a Russian tanning too, still you can get through it. Only, mind my step-mother Elenorka's nowhere about! Dad's afraid of her, and she wants to keep everything for her brats! But there, you know your way about! Good-bye!'

'Ugh, what a low beast that boy is!' cried Fustov, as soon as the door had slammed-to.

His face was burning, as though from the fire, and he turned away from me. I did not question him, and soon retired.

XII

All that day I spent in speculating about Fustov, about Susanna, and about her relations. I had a vague feeling of something like a family drama. As far as I could judge, my friend was not indifferent to Susanna. But she? Did she care for him? Why did she seem so unhappy? And altogether, what sort of creature was she? These questions were continually recurring to my mind. An obscure but strong conviction told me that it would be no use to apply to Fustov for the solution of them. It ended in my setting off the next day alone to Mr. Ratsch's house.

I felt all at once very uncomfortable and confused directly I found myself in the dark little passage. 'She won't appear even, very likely,' flashed into my mind. 'I shall have to stop with the repulsive veteran and his cook of a wife.... And indeed, even if she does show herself, what of it? She won't even take part in the conversation.... She was anything but warm in her manner to me the other day. Why ever did I come?' While I was making these reflections, the little page ran to announce my presence, and in the adjoining room, after two or three wondering 'Who is it? Who, do you say?' I heard the heavy shuffling of slippers, the folding-door was slightly opened, and in the crack between its two halves was thrust the face of Ivan Demianitch, an unkempt and grim-looking face. It stared at me and its expression did not immediately change.... Evidently, Mr. Ratsch did not at once recognise me; but suddenly his cheeks grew rounder, his eyes narrower, and from his opening mouth, there burst, together with a guffaw, the exclamation: 'Ah! my dear sir! Is it you? Pray walk in!'

I followed him all the more unwillingly, because it seemed to me that this affable, good-humoured Mr. Ratsch was inwardly wishing me at the devil. There was nothing to be done, however. He led me into the drawing-room, and in the drawing-room who should be sitting but Susanna, bending over an account-book? She glanced at me with her melancholy eyes, and very slightly bit the finger-nails of her left hand.... It was a habit of hers, I noticed, a habit peculiar to nervous people. There was no one else in the room.

'You see, sir,' began Mr. Ratsch, dealing himself a smack on the haunch, 'what you've found Susanna Ivanovna and me busy upon: we're at our accounts. My spouse has no great head for arithmetic and I, I must own, try to spare my eyes. I can't read without spectacles, what am I to do? Let the young people exert themselves, ha-ha! That's the proper thing. But there's no need of haste.... More haste, worse speed in catching fleas, he-he!'

Susanna closed the book and was about to leave the room.

'Wait a bit, wait a bit,' began Mr. Ratsch. 'It's no great matter if you're not in your best dress....' (Susanna was wearing a very old, almost childish, frock with short sleeves.) 'Our dear guest is not a stickler for ceremony, and I should like just to clear up last week.... You don't mind?'—he addressed me. 'We needn't stand on ceremony with you, eh?'

'Please don't put yourself out on my behalf!' I cried.

'To be sure, my good friend. As you're aware, the late Tsar Alexey Nikolavitch Romanoff used to say, "Time is for business, but a minute for recreation!" We'll devote one minute only to that same business... ha-ha! What about that thirteen roubles and thirty kopecks?' he added in a low voice, turning his back on me.

'Viktor took it from Eleonora Karpovna; he said that it was with your leave,' Susanna replied, also in a low voice.

'He said... he said... my leave...' growled Ivan Demianitch. 'I'm on the spot myself, I fancy. Might be asked. And who's had that seventeen roubles?'

'The upholsterer.'

'Oh... the upholster. What's that for?' 'His bill.'

'His bill. Show me!' He pulled the book away from Susanna, and planting a pair of round spectacles with silver rims on his nose, he began passing his finger along the lines. 'The upholsterer,.. the upholsterer...You'd chuck all the money out of doors! Nothing pleases you better!...Wie die Croaten! A bill indeed! But, after all,' he added aloud, and he turned round facing me again, and pulled the spectacles off his nose, 'why do this now? I can go into these wretched details later. Susanna Ivanovna, be so good as to put away that account-book, and come back to us and enchant our kind guest's ears with your musical accomplishments, to wit, playing on the piano forte... Eh?'

Susanna turned her head away.

'I should be very happy,' I hastily observed; 'it would be a great pleasure for me to hear Susanna Ivanovna play. But I would not for anything in the world be a trouble...'

'Trouble, indeed, what nonsense! Now then, Susanna Ivanovna, eins, zwei, drei!'

Susanna made no response and went out.

XIII

I had not expected her to come back; but she quickly reappeared. She had not even changed her dress, and sitting down in a corner, she looked twice intently at me. Whether it was that she was conscious in my manner to her of the involuntary respect, inexplicable to myself, which, more than curiosity, more even than sympathy, she aroused in me, or whether she was in a softened frame of mind that day, anyway, she suddenly went to the piano, and laying her hand irresolutely on the keys, and turning her head a little over her shoulder towards me, she asked what I would like her to play. Before I had time to answer she had seated herself, taken up some music, hurriedly opened it, and begun to play. I loved music from childhood, but at that time I had but little comprehension of it, and very slight knowledge of the works of the great masters, and if Mr. Ratsch had not grumbled with some dissatisfaction, 'Aha! wieder dieser Beethoven!' I should not have guessed what Susanna had chosen. It was, as I found out afterwards, the celebrated sonata in F minor, opus 57. Susanna's playing impressed me more than I can say, I had not expected such force, such fire, such bold execution. At the very first bars of the intensely passionate allegro, the beginning of the sonata, I felt that numbness, that chill and sweet terror of ecstasy, which instantaneously enwrap the soul when beauty bursts with sudden flight upon it. I did not stir a limb till the very end. I kept, wanting—and not daring—to sigh. I was sitting behind Susanna; I could not see her face; I saw only from time to time her long dark hair tossed up and down on her shoulders, her figure swaying impulsively, and her delicate arms and bare elbows swiftly, and rather angularly, moving. The last notes died away. I sighed at last. Susanna still sat before the piano.

'Ja, ja,' observed Mr. Ratsch, who had also, however, listened with attention; 'romantische Musik! That's all the fashion nowadays. Only, why not play correctly? Eh? Put your finger on two notes at once—what's that for? Eh? To be sure, all we care for is to go quickly, quickly! Turns it out hotter, eh? Hot pancakes!' he bawled like a street seller.

Susanna turned slightly towards Mr. Ratsch. I caught sight of her face in profile. The delicate eyebrow rose high above the downcast eyelid, an unsteady flush overspread the cheek, the little ear was red under the lock pushed behind it.

'I have heard all the best performers with my own ears,' pursued Mr. Ratsch, suddenly frowning, 'and compared with the late Field they were all—tfoo! nil! zero!! Das war ein Kerl! Und ein so reines Spiel! And his own compositions the finest things! But all those now "tloo-too-too," and "tra-ta-ta," are written, I suppose, more for beginners. Da braucht man keine Delicatesse! Bang the keys anyhow... no matter! It'll turn out somehow! Janitscharen Musik! Pugh!' (Ivan Demianitch wiped his forehead with his handkerchief.) 'But I don't say that for you, Susanna Ivanovna; you played well, and oughtn't to be hurt by my remarks.'

'Everyone has his own taste,' Susanna said in a low voice, and her lips were trembling; 'but your remarks, Ivan Demianitch, you know, cannot hurt me.'

'Oh! of course not! Only don't you imagine'—Mr. Ratsch turned to me—'don't you imagine, my young friend, that that comes from our excessive good-nature and meekness of spirit; it's simply that we fancy ourselves so highly exalted that—oo-oo!—we can't keep our cap on our head, as the Russian proverb says, and, of course, no criticism can touch us. The conceit, my dear sir, the conceit!'

I listened in surprise to Mr. Ratsch. Spite, the bitterest spite, seemed as if it were boiling over in every word he uttered.... And long it must have been rankling! It choked him. He tried to conclude his tirade with his usual laugh, and fell into a husky, broken cough instead. Susanna did not let drop a syllable in reply to him, only she shook her head, raised her face, and clasping her elbows with her hands, stared straight at him. In the depths of her fixed, wide-open eyes the hatred of long years lay smouldering with dim, unquenchable fire. I felt ill at ease.

'You belong to two different musical generations,' I began, with an effort at lightness, wishing by this lightness to suggest that I noticed nothing, 'and so it is not surprising that you do not agree in your opinions.... But, Ivan Demianitch, you must allow me to take rather... the side of the younger generation. I'm an outsider, of course; but I must confess nothing in music has ever made such an impression on me as the... as what Susanna Ivanovna has just played us.'

Ratsch pounced at once upon me.

'And what makes you suppose,' he roared, still purple from the fit of coughing, 'that we want to enlist you on our side? We don't want that at all! Freedom for the free, salvation for the saved! But as to the two generations, that's right enough; we old folks find it hard to get on with you young people, very hard! Our ideas don't agree in anything: neither in art, nor in life, nor even in morals; do they, Susanna Ivanovna?'

Susanna smiled a contemptuous smile.

'Especially in regard to morals, as you say, our ideas do not agree, and cannot agree,' she responded, and something menacing seemed to flit over her brows, while her lips were faintly trembling as before.

'Of course! of course!' Ratsch broke in, 'I'm not a philosopher! I'm not capable of... rising so superior! I'm a plain man, swayed by prejudices—oh yes!'

Susanna smiled again.

'I think, Ivan Demianitch, you too have sometimes been able to place yourself above what are called prejudices.'

'Wie so? How so, I mean? I don't know what you mean.'

'You don't know what I mean? Your memory's so bad!'

Mr. Ratsch seemed utterly taken aback.

'I... I...' he repeated, 'I...'

'Yes, you, Mr. Ratsch.'

There followed a brief silence.

'Really, upon my word...' Mr. Ratsch was beginning; 'how dare you... such insolence...'

Susanna all at once drew herself up to her full height, and still holding her elbows, squeezing them tight, drumming on them with her fingers, she stood still facing Ratsch. She seemed to challenge him to conflict, to stand up to meet him. Her face was changed; it became suddenly, in one instant, extraordinarily beautiful, and terrible too; a sort of bright, cold brilliance—the brilliance of steel—gleamed in her lustreless eyes; the lips that had been quivering were compressed in one straight, mercilessly stern line. Susanna challenged Ratsch, but he gazed blankly, and suddenly subsiding into silence, all of a heap, so to say, drew his head in, even stepped back a pace. The veteran of the year twelve was afraid; there could be no mistake about that.

Susanna slowly turned her eyes from him to me, as though calling upon me to witness her victory, and the humiliation of her foe, and, smiling once more, she walked out of the room.

The veteran remained a little while motionless in his arm-chair; at last, as though recollecting a forgotten part, he roused himself, got up and slapping me on the shoulder, laughed his noisy guffaw.

'There, 'pon my soul! fancy now, it's over ten years since I've been living with that young lady, and yet she never can see when I'm joking, and when I'm in earnest! And you too, my young friend, are a little puzzled, I do believe.... Ha-ha-ha! That's because you don't know old Ratsch!'

'No.... I do know you now,' I thought, not without a feeling of some alarm and disgust.

'You don't know the old fellow, you don't know him,' he repeated, stroking himself on the stomach, as he accompanied me into the passage. 'I may be a tiresome person, knocked about by life, ha-ha! But I'm a good-hearted fellow, 'pon my soul, I am!'

I rushed headlong from the stairs into the street. I longed with all speed to get away from that good-hearted fellow.

XIV

'They hate one another, that's clear,' I thought, as I returned homewards; 'there's no doubt either that he's a wretch of a man, and she's a good girl. But what has there been between them? What is the reason of this continual exasperation? What was the meaning of those hints? And how suddenly it broke out! On such a trivial pretext!'

Next day Fustov and I had arranged to go to the theatre, to see Shtchepkin in 'Woe from Wit.' Griboyedov's comedy had only just been licensed for performance after being first disfigured by the censors' mutilations. We warmly applauded Famusov and Skalozub. I don't remember what actor took the part of Tchatsky, but I well remember that he was indescribably bad. He made his first appearance in a Hungarian jacket, and boots with tassels, and came on later in a frockcoat of the colour 'flamme du punch,' then in fashion, and the frockcoat looked about as suitable as it would have done on our old butler. I recollect too that we were all in ecstasies over the ball in the third act. Though, probably, no one ever executed such steps in reality, it was accepted as correct, and I believe it is acted in just the same way today. One of the guests hopped excessively high, while his wig flew from side to side, and the public roared with laughter. As we were coming out of the theatre, we jostled against Viktor in a corridor.

'You were in the theatre!' he cried, flinging his arms about. 'How was it I didn't see you? I'm awfully glad I met you. You must come and have supper with me. Come on; I'll stand the supper!'

Young Ratsch seemed in an excited, almost ecstatic, frame of mind. His little eyes darted to and fro; he was grinning, and there were spots of red on his face.

'Why this gleefulness?' asked Fustov.

'Why? Wouldn't you like to know, eh?' Viktor drew us a little aside, and pulling out of his trouser-pocket a whole bundle of the red and blue notes then in use waved them in the air.

Fustov was surprised.

'Has your governor been so liberal?'

Viktor chuckled.

'He liberal! You just try it on!... This morning, relying on your intercession, I asked him for cash. What do you suppose the old skinflint answered? "I'll pay your debts," he says, "if you like. Up to twenty-five roubles inclusive!" Do you hear, inclusive! No, sir, this was a gift from God in my destitution. A lucky chance.'

'Been robbing someone?' Fustov hazarded carelessly.

Viktor frowned.

'Robbing, not indeed! I won it, won it from an officer, a guardsman. He only arrived from Petersburg yesterday. Such a chain of circumstances! It's worth telling... only this isn't the place. Come along to Yar's, not a couple of steps. I'll stand the show, as I said!'

We ought, perhaps, to have refused; but we followed without making any objection.

XV

At Yar's we were shown into a private room; supper was served, champagne was brought. Viktor related to us, omitting no detail, how he had in a certain 'gay' house met this officer of the guards, a very nice chap and of good family, only without a hap'orth of brains; how they had made friends, how he, the officer that is, had suggested as a joke a game of 'fools' with Viktor with some old cards, for next to nothing, and with the condition that the officer's winnings should go to the benefit of Wilhelmina, but Viktor's to his own benefit; how afterwards they had got on to betting on the games.

'And I, and I,' cried Viktor, and he jumped up and clapped his hands, 'I hadn't more than six roubles in my pocket all the while. Fancy! And at first I was completely cleaned out.... A nice position! Only then—in answer to whose prayers I can't say—fortune smiled. The other fellow began to get hot and kept showing all his cards.... In no time he'd lost seven hundred and fifty roubles! He began begging me to go on playing, but I'm not quite a fool, I fancy; no, one mustn't abuse such luck; I popped on my hat and cut away. So now I've no need to eat humble pie with the governor and can treat my friends.... Hi waiter! Another bottle! Gentlemen, let's clink glasses!'

We did clink glasses with Viktor, and continued drinking and laughing with him, though his story was by no means to our liking, nor was his society a source of any great satisfaction to us either. He began being very affable, playing the buffoon, unbending, in fact, and was more loathsome than ever. Viktor noticed at last the impression he was making on us and began to get sulky; his remarks became more disconnected and his looks gloomier. He began yawning, announced that he was sleepy, and after swearing with his characteristic coarseness at the waiter for a badly cleaned pipe, he suddenly accosted Fustov, with a challenging expression on his distorted face.

'I say, Alexander Daviditch,' he said, 'you tell me, if you please, what do you look down on me for?'

'How so?' My friend was momentarily at a loss for a reply.

'I'll tell you how.... I'm very well aware that you look down on me, and that person does too' (he pointed at me with his finger), 'so there! As though you were yourself remarkable for such high and exalted principles and weren't just as much a sinner as the rest of us. Worse even. Still waters... you know the proverb?'

Fustov turned rather red.

'What do you mean by that?' he asked.

'Why, I mean that I'm not blind yet, and I see very clearly everything that's going on under my nose.... And I have nothing against it: first it's not my principle to interfere, and secondly, my sister Susanna Ivanovna hasn't always been so exemplary herself.... Only, why look down on me?'

'You don't understand what you're babbling there yourself! You're drunk,' said Fustov, taking his overcoat from the wall. 'He's swindled some fool of his money, and now he's telling all sorts of lies!'

Viktor continued reclining on the sofa, and merely swung his legs, which were hanging over its arm.

'Swindled! Why did you drink the wine then? It was paid for with the money I won, you know. As for lies, I've no need for lying. It's not my fault that in her past Susanna Ivanovna...'

'Hold your tongue!' Fustov shouted at him, 'hold your tongue... or...'

'Or what?'

'You'll find out what. Come along, Piotr.'

'Aha!' pursued Viktor; 'our noble-hearted knight takes refuge in flight. He doesn't care to hear the truth, that's evident! It stings—the truth does, it seems!'

'Come along, Piotr,' Fustov repeated, completely losing his habitual coolness and self-possession.

'Let's leave this wretch of a boy!'

'The boy's not afraid of you, do you hear,' Viktor shouted after us, 'he despises you, the boy does! Do you hear!'

Fustov walked so quickly along the street that I had difficulty in keeping up with him. All at once he stopped short and turned sharply back.

'Where are you going?' I asked.

'Oh, I must find out what the idiot.... He's drunk, no doubt, God knows what.... Only don't you follow me... we shall see each other tomorrow. Good-bye!'

And hurriedly pressing my hand, Fustov set off towards Yar's hotel.

Next day I missed seeing Fustov; and on the day after that, ongoing to his rooms, I learned that he had gone into the country to his uncle's, near Moscow. I inquired if he had left no note for me, but no note was forth-coming. Then I asked the servant whether he knew how long Alexander Daviditch would be away in the country. 'A fortnight, or a little more, probably,' replied the man. I took at any rate Fustov's exact address, and sauntered home, meditating deeply. This unexpected absence from Moscow, in the winter, completed my utter perplexity. My good aunt observed to me at dinner that I seemed continually expecting something and gazed at the cabbage pie as though I were beholding it for the first time in my life. 'Pierre, vous n'êtes pas amoureux?' she cried at last, having previously got rid of her companions. But I reassured her: no, I was not in love.

XVI

Three days passed. I had a secret prompting to go to the Ratschs'. I fancied that in their house I should be sure to find a solution of all that absorbed my mind, that I could not make out.... But I should have had to meet the veteran.... That thought pulled me up. One tempestuous evening—the February wind was howling angrily outside, the frozen snow tapped at the window from time to time like coarse sand flung by a mighty hand—I was sitting in my room, trying to read. My servant came, and, with a mysterious air, announced that a lady wished to see me. I was surprised... ladies did not visit me, especially at such a late hour; however, I told him to show her in. The door opened and with swift step there walked in a woman, muffled up in a light summer cloak and a yellow shawl. Abruptly she cast off the cloak and the shawl, which were covered with snow, and I saw standing before me Susanna. I was so astonished that I did not utter a word, while she went up to the window, and leaning her shoulder against the wall, remained motionless; only her bosom heaved convulsively and her eyes moved restlessly, and the breath came with a faint moan from her white lips. I realised that it was no slight trouble that had brought her to me; I realised, for all my youth and shallowness, that at that instant before my eyes the fate of a whole life was being decided—a bitter and terrible fate.

'Susanna Ivanovna,' I began, 'how...'

She suddenly clutched my hand in her icy fingers, but her voice failed her. She gave a broken sigh and looked down. Her heavy coils of black hair fell about her face.... The snow had not melted from off it.

'Please, calm yourself, sit down,' I began again, 'see here, on the sofa. What has happened? Sit down, I entreat you.'

'No,' she articulated, scarcely audibly, and she sank on to the window-seat. 'I am all right here.... Let me be.... You could not expect... but if you knew... if I could... if...'

She tried to control herself, but the tears flowed from her eyes with a violence that shook her, and sobs, hurried, devouring sobs, filled the room. I felt a tightness at my heart.... I was utterly stupefied. I had seen Susanna only twice; I had conjectured that she had a hard life, but

I had regarded her as a proud girl, of strong character, and all at once these violent, despairing tears.... Mercy! Why, one only weeps like that in the presence of death!

I stood like one condemned to death myself.

'Excuse me,' she said at last, several times, almost angrily, wiping first one eye, then the other. 'It'll soon be over. I've come to see you....' She was still sobbing, but without tears. 'I've come.... You know that Alexander Daviditch has gone away?'

In this single question Susanna revealed everything, and she glanced at me, as though she would say: 'You understand, of course, you will have pity, won't you?' Unhappy girl! There was no other course left her then!

I did not know what answer to make....

'He has gone away; he has gone away... he believed him!' Susanna was saying meanwhile. 'He did not care even to question me; he thought I should not tell him all the truth; he could think that of me! As though I had ever deceived him!'

She bit her lower lip, and bending a little, began to scratch with her nail the patterns of ice that covered the window-pane. I went hastily into the next room, and sending my servant away, came back at once and lighted another candle. I had no clear idea why I was doing all this.... I was greatly overcome. Susanna was sitting as before on the window-seat, and it was at this moment that I noticed how lightly she was dressed: a grey gown with white buttons and a broad leather belt, that was all. I went up to her, but she did not take any notice of me.

'He believed it,... he believed it,' she whispered, swaying softly from side to side. 'He did not hesitate; he dealt me this last... last blow!' She turned suddenly to me. 'You know his address?'

'Yes, Susanna Ivanovna.. I learnt it from his servants... at his house. He told me nothing of his intention; I had not seen him for two days—went to inquire and he had already left Moscow.'

'You know his address?' she repeated. 'Well, write to him then that he has killed me. You are a good man, I know. He did not talk to you of me, I dare say, but he talked to me about you. Write... ah, write to him to come back quickly, if he wants to find me alive!... No! He will not find me!...'

Susanna's voice grew quieter at each word, and she was quieter altogether. But this calm seemed to me more awful than the previous sobs.

'He believed him,...' she said again, and rested her chin on her clasped hands.

A sudden squall of wind beat upon the window with a sharp whistle and a thud of snow. A cold draught passed over the room.... The candles flickered.... Susanna shivered. Again, I begged her to sit on the sofa.

'No, no, let me be,' she answered, 'I am all right here. Please.' She huddled up to the frozen pane, as though she had found herself a refuge in the recesses of the window. 'Please.'

'But you're shivering, you're frozen,' I cried, 'Look, your shoes are soaked.'

'Let me be... please...' she whispered,. and closed her eyes.

A panic seized me.

'Susanna Ivanovna!' I almost screamed: 'do rouse yourself, I entreat you! What is the matter with you? Why such despair? You will see, everything will be cleared up, some misunderstanding... some unlooked-for chance.... You will see, he will soon be back. I will let him know.... I will write to him today.... But I will not repeat your words.... Is it possible!'

'He will not find me,' Susanna murmured, still in the same subdued voice. 'Do you suppose I would have come here, to you, to a stranger, if I had not known I should not long be living? Ah, all my past has been swept away beyond return! You see, I could not bear to die so, in solitude, in silence, without saying to someone, "I've lost everything... and I'm dying.... Look!"'

She drew back into her cold little corner.... Never shall I forget that head, those fixed eyes with their deep, burnt-out look, those dark, disordered tresses against the pale window-pane, even the grey, narrow gown, under every fold of which throbbed such a young, passionate life!

Unconsciously I flung up my hands.

'You... you die, Susanna Ivanovna! You have only to live.... You must live!'

She looked at me.... My words seemed to surprise her.

'Ah, you don't know,' she began, and she softly dropped both her hands. 'I cannot live, Too much, too much I have had to suffer, too much! I lived through it.... I hoped... but now... when even this is shattered... when...'

She raised her eyes to the ceiling and seemed to sink into thought. The tragic line, which I had once noticed about her lips, came out now still more clearly; it seemed to spread across her whole face. It seemed as though some relentless hand had drawn it immutably, had set a mark for ever on this lost soul.

She was still silent.

'Susanna Ivanovna,' I said, to break that awful silence with anything; 'he will come back, I assure you!'

Susanna looked at me again.

'What do you say?' she enunciated with visible effort.

'He will come back, Susanna Ivanovna, Alexander will come back!'

'He will come back?' she repeated. 'But even if he did come back, I cannot forgive him this humiliation, this lack of faith....'

She clutched at her head.

'My God! my God! what am I saying, and why am I here? What is it all? What... what did I come to ask... and whom? Ah, I am going mad!...'

Her eyes came to a rest.

'You wanted to ask me to write to Alexander,' I made haste to remind her.

She started.

'Yes, write, write to him... what you like.... And here...' She hurriedly fumbled in her pocket and brought out a little manuscript book. 'This

I was writing for him... before he ran away.... But he believed... he believed him!'

I understood that her words referred to Viktor; Susanna would not mention him, would not utter his detested name.

'But, Susanna Ivanovna, excuse me,' I began, 'what makes you suppose that Alexander Daviditch had any conversation... with that person?'

'What? Why, he himself came to me and told me all about it and bragged of it... and laughed just as his father laughs! Here, here, take it,' she went on, thrusting the manuscript into my hand, 'read it, send it to him, burn it, throw it away, do what you like, as you please.... But I can't die like this with no one knowing.... Now it is time.... I must go.'

She got up from the window-seat.... I stopped her.

'Where are you going, Susanna Ivanovna, mercy on us! Listen, what a storm is raging! You are so lightly dressed.... And your home is not near here. Let me at least go for a carriage, for a sledge....'

'No, no, I want nothing,' she said resolutely, repelling me and taking up her cloak and shawl. 'Don't keep me, for God's sake! or... I can't answer for anything! I feel an abyss, a dark abyss under my feet.... Don't come near me, don't touch me!' With feverish haste she put on her cloak, arranged her shawl.... 'Good-bye... good-bye.... Oh, my unhappy people, forever strangers, a curse lies upon us! No one has ever cared for me, was it likely he...' She suddenly ceased. 'No; one man loved me,' she began again, wringing her hands, 'but death is all about me, death and no escape! Now it is my turn.... Don't come after me,' she cried shrilly. 'Don't come! don't come!'

I was petrified, while she rushed out; and an instant later, I heard the slam downstairs of the heavy street door, and the windowpanes shook again under the violent onslaught of the blast.

I could not quickly recover myself. I was only beginning life in those days: I had had no experience of passion nor of suffering and had rarely witnessed any manifestation of strong feeling in others.... But the sincerity of this suffering, of this passion, impressed me. If it had not been for the manuscript in my hands, I might have thought that I had dreamed it all—it was all so unlikely, and swooped by like a passing storm. I was reading the manuscript till midnight. It consisted of several sheets of letter-paper, closely covered with a large, irregular writing, almost without an erasure. Not a single line was quite straight, and one seemed in every one of them to feel the excited trembling of the hand that held the pen. Here follows what was in the manuscript. I have kept it to this day.

XVII

MY STORY

I am twenty-eight years old this year. Here are my earliest recollections; I was living in the Tambov province, in the country house of a rich landowner, Ivan Matveitch Koltovsky, in a small room on the second storey. With me lived my mother, a Jewess, daughter of a dead painter, who had come from abroad, a woman always ailing, with an extraordinarily beautiful face, pale as wax, and such mournful eyes, that sometimes when she gazed long at me, even without looking at her, I was aware of her sorrowful, sorrowful eyes, and I would burst into tears and rush to embrace her. I had tutors come to me; I had music lessons and was called 'miss.' I dined at the master's table together with my mother. Mr. Koltovsky was a tall, handsome old man with a stately manner; he always smelt of *ambre*. I stood in mortal terror of him, though he called me Suzon and gave me his dry, sinewy hand to kiss under its lace-ruffles. With my mother he was elaborately courteous, but he talked little even with her. He would say two or three affable words, to which she promptly made a hurried answer; and he would be silent and sit looking about him with dignity, and slowly picking up a pinch of Spanish snuff from his round, golden snuff-box with the arms of the Empress Catherine on it.

My ninth year has always remained vivid in my memory.... I learnt then, from the maids in the servants' room, that Ivan Matveitch Koltovsky was my father, and almost on the same day, my mother, by his command, was married to Mr. Ratsch, who was something like a steward to him. I was utterly unable to comprehend the possibility of such a thing, I was bewildered, I was almost ill, my brain suffered under the strain, my mind was overclouded. 'Is it true, is it true, mamma,' I asked her, 'that scented bogey' (that was my name for Ivan Matveitch) 'is my father?' My mother was terribly scared, she shut my mouth.... 'Never speak to any one of that, do you hear, Susanna, do you hear, not a word!'... she repeated in a shaking voice, pressing my head to her bosom.... And I never did speak to anyone of it.... That prohibition of my mother's I understood.... I understood that I must be silent, that my mother begged my forgiveness!

My unhappiness began from that day. Mr. Ratsch did not love my mother, and she did not love him. He married her for money, and she was obliged to submit. Mr. Koltovsky probably considered that in this way everything had been arranged for the best, *la position était régularisée*. I remember the day before the marriage my mother and I—both locked in each other's arms—wept almost the whole morning—bitterly, bitterly—and silently. It is not strange that she was silent.... What could she say to me? But that I did not question her shows that unhappy children learn wisdom sooner than happy ones... to their cost.

Mr. Koltovsky continued to interest himself in my education, and even by degrees put me on a more intimate footing. He did not talk to me... but morning and evening, after flicking the snuff from his jabot with two fingers, he would with the same two fingers—always icy cold—pat me on the cheek and give me some sort of dark-coloured sweetmeats, also smelling of *ambre*, which I never ate. At twelve years old I became his reader—-*sa petite lectrice*. I read him French books of the last century, the memoirs of Saint Simon, of Mably, Renal, Helvetius, Voltaire's correspondence, the encyclopedists, of course without understanding a word, even when, with a smile and a grimace, he ordered me, 'relire ce dernier paragraphe, qui est bien remarquable!' Ivan Matveitch was completely a Frenchman. He had lived in Paris till the Revolution, remembered Marie Antoinette, and had received an invitation to Trianon to see her. He had also seen Mirabeau, who, according to his account, wore very large buttons—*exagéré en tout*, and was altogether a man of *mauvais ton, en dépit de sa naissance!* Ivan Matveitch, however, rarely talked of that time; but two or three times a year, addressing himself to the crooked old emigrant whom he had taken into his house and called for some unknown reason

'M. le Commandeur,' he recited in his deliberate, nasal voice, the impromptu he had once delivered at a soiree of the Duchesse de Polignac. I remember only the first two lines.... It had reference to a comparison between the Russians and the French:

'L'aigle se plait aux regions austères

Ou le ramier ne saurait habiter...'

'Digne de M. de Saint Aulaire!' M. le Commandeur would exclaim every time.

Ivan Matveitch looked youngish up to the time of his death: his cheeks were rosy, his teeth white, his eyebrows thick and immobile, his eyes agreeable and expressive, clear, black eyes, perfect agate. He was not at all unreasonable and was very courteous with everyone, even with the servants.... But my God! how wretched I was with him, with what joy I always left him, what evil thoughts confounded me in his presence! Ah, I was not to blame for them!... I was not to blame for what they had made of me....

Mr. Ratsch was, after his marriage, assigned a lodge not far from the big house. I lived there with my mother. It was a cheerless life I led there. She soon gave birth to a son, Viktor, this same Viktor whom I have every right to think and to call my enemy. From the time of his birth my mother never regained her health, which had always been weak. Mr. Ratsch did not think fit in those days to keep up such a show of good spirits as he maintains now: he always wore a morose air and tried to pass for a busy, hard-working person. To me he was cruel and rude. I felt relief when I retired from Ivan Matveitch's presence; but my own home too I was glad to leave.... Unhappy was my youth! Forever tossed from one shore to the other, with no desire to anchor at either! I would run across the courtyard in winter, through the deep snow, in a thin frock—run to the big house to read to Ivan Matveitch and as it were be glad to go.... But when I was there, when I saw those great cheerless rooms, the bright-coloured, upholstered furniture, that courteous and heartless old man in the open silk wadded jacket, in the white jabot and white cravat, with lace ruffles falling over his fingers, with a *soupçon* of powder (so his valet expressed it) on his combed-back hair, I felt choked by the stifling scent of *ambre*, and my heart sank. Ivan Matveitch usually sat in a large low chair; on the wall behind his head hung a picture, representing a young woman, with a bright and bold expression of face, dressed in a sumptuous Hebrew costume, and simply covered with precious stones, with diamonds.... I often stole a glance at this picture, but only later on I learned that it was the portrait of my mother, painted by her father at Ivan Matveitch's request. She had changed indeed since those days! Well had he succeeded in subduing and crushing her! 'And she loved him! Loved that old man!' was my thought.... 'How could it be! Love him!' And yet, when I recalled some of my mother's glances, some half-uttered phrases and unconscious gestures.... 'Yes, yes, she did love him!' I repeated with horror. Ah, God, spare others from knowing aught of such feelings!

Every day I read to Ivan Matveitch, sometimes for three or four hours together.... So much reading in such a loud voice was harmful to me. Our doctor was anxious about my lungs and even once communicated his fears to Ivan Matveitch. But the old man only smiled—no; he never smiled, but somehow sharpened and moved forward his lips—and told him: 'Vous ne savez pas ce qu'il y a de ressources dans cette jeunesse.' 'In former years, however, M. le Commandeur,'... the doctor ventured to observe. Ivan Matveitch smiled as before. 'Vous rêvez, mon cher,' he interposed: 'le commandeur n'a plus de dents, et il crache à chaque mot. J'aime les voix jeunes.'

And I still went on reading, though my cough was very troublesome in the mornings and at night.... Sometimes Ivan Matveitch made me play the piano. But music always had a soporific influence on his nerves. His eyes closed at once, his head nodded in time, and only rarely I heard, 'C'est du Steibelt, n'est-ce pas? Jouez-moi du Steibelt!' Ivan Matveitch looked upon Steibelt as a great genius, who had succeeded in overcoming in himself 'la grossière lourdeur des Allemands,' and only found fault with him for one thing: 'trop de fougue! trop d'imagination!'... When Ivan Matveitch noticed that I was tired from playing he would offer me 'du cachou de Bologne.' So, day after day slipped by....

And then one night—a night never to be forgotten!—a terrible calamity fell upon me. My mother died almost suddenly. I was only fifteen. Oh, what a sorrow that was, with what cruel violence it swooped down upon me! How terrified I was at that first meeting with death! My poor mother! Strange were our relations; we passionately loved each other... passionately and hopelessly; we both as it were treasured up and hid from each other our common secret, kept obstinately silent about it, though we knew all that was passing at the bottom of our hearts! Even of the past, of her own early past, my mother never spoke to me, and she never complained in words, though her whole being was nothing but one dumb complaint. We avoided all conversation of any seriousness. Alas! I kept hoping that the time would come, and she would open her heart at last, and I too should speak out, and both of us would be more at ease.... But the little daily cares, her irresolute, shrinking temper, illnesses, the presence of Mr. Ratsch, and most of all the eternal question,—what is the use? and the relentless, unbroken flowing away of time, of life.... All was ended as though by a clap of thunder, and the words which would have loosed us from the burden of our secret—even the last dying words of leave-taking—I was not destined to hear from my mother! All that is left in my memory is Mr. Ratsch's calling, 'Susanna Ivanovna, go, please, your mother wishes to give you her blessing!' and then the pale hand stretched out from the heavy counterpane, the agonised breathing, the dying eyes.... Oh, enough! enough!

With what horror, with what indignation and piteous curiosity I looked the next day, and on the day of the funeral, into the face of my father... yes, my father! In my dead mother's writing-case his letters were found. I fancied he looked a little pale and drawn... but no! Nothing was stirring in that heart of stone. Exactly as before, he summoned me to his room, a week later; exactly in the same voice he asked me to read: 'Si vous le voulez bien, les observations sur l'histoire de France de Mably, à la page 74... là où nous avons ètè interrompus.' And he had not even had my mother's portrait moved! On dismissing me, he did indeed call me to him and giving me his hand to kiss a second time, he observed: 'Suzanne, la mort de votre mère vous a privée de votre appui naturel; mais vous pourrez toujours compter sur ma protection,' but with the other hand he gave me at once a slight push on the shoulder, and, with the sharpening of the corners of the mouth habitual with him, he added, 'Allez, mon enfant.' I longed to shriek at him: 'Why, but you know you're my father!' but I said nothing and left the room.

Next morning, early, I went to the graveyard. May had come in all its glory of flowers and leaves, and a long while I sat on the new grave. I did not weep, nor grieve; one thought was filling my brain: 'Do you hear, mother? He means to extend his protection to me, too!' And it seemed to me that my mother ought not to be wounded by the smile which it instinctively called up on my lips.

At times I wonder what made me so persistently desire to wring—not a confession... No, indeed! but, at least, one warm word of kinship from Ivan Matveitch? Didn't I know what he was and how little he was like all that I pictured in my dreams as a *father*!... But I was so lonely, so alone on earth! And then, that thought, ever recurring, gave me no rest: 'Did she not love him? She must have loved him for something?'

Three years more slipped by. Nothing changed in the monotonous round of life, marked out and arranged for us. Viktor was growing into a boy. I was eight years older and would gladly have looked after him, but Mr. Ratsch opposed my doing so. He gave him a nurse, who had orders to keep strict watch that the child was not 'spoilt,' that is, not to allow me to go near him. And Viktor himself fought shy of me. One day Mr. Ratsch came into my room, perturbed, excited, and angry. On the previous evening unpleasant rumours had reached me about my stepfather; the servants were talking of his having been caught embezzling a considerable sum of money and taking bribes from a merchant.

'You can assist me,' he began, tapping impatiently on the table with his fingers. 'Go and speak for me to Ivan Matveitch.'

'Speak for you? On what ground? What about?'

'Intercede for me.... I'm not like a stranger anyway... I'm accused... well, the fact is, I may be left without bread to eat, and you, too.'

'But how can I go to him? How can I disturb him?'

'What next! You have a right to disturb him!'

'What right, Ivan Demianitch?'

'Come, no humbug.... He cannot refuse you, for many reasons. Do you mean to tell me you don't understand that?'

He looked insolently into my eyes, and I felt my cheeks simply burning. Hatred, contempt, rose up within me, surged in a rush upon me, drowning me.

'Yes, I understand you, Ivan Demianitch,' I answered at last—my own voice seemed strange to me—'and I am not going to Ivan Matveitch, and I will not ask him for anything. Bread, or no bread!'

Mr. Ratsch shivered, ground his teeth, and clenched his fists.

'All right, wait a bit, your highness!' he muttered huskily. 'I won't forget it!' That same day, Ivan Matveitch sent for him, and, I was told, shook his cane at him, the very cane which he had once exchanged with the Due de la Rochefoucauld, and cried, 'You be a scoundrel and extortioner! I put you outside!' Ivan Matveitch could hardly speak Russian at all, and despised our 'coarse jargon,' *ce jargon vulgaire et rude*. Someone once said before him, 'That same's self-understood.' Ivan Matveitch was quite indignant, and often afterwards quoted the phrase as an example of the senselessness and absurdity of the Russian tongue. 'What does it mean, that same's self-understood?' he would ask in Russian, with emphasis on each syllable. 'Why not simply that's understood, and why same and self?'

Ivan Matveitch did not, however, dismiss Mr. Ratsch, he did not even deprive him of his position. But my stepfather kept his word: he never forgot it.

I began to notice a change in Ivan Matveitch. He was low-spirited, depressed, his health broke down a little. His fresh, rosy face grew yellow and wrinkled; he lost a front tooth. He quite ceased going out and gave up the reception-days he had established for the peasants, without the assistance of the priest, *sans le concours du clergé*. On such days Ivan Matveitch had been in the habit of going in to the peasants in the hall or on the balcony, with a rose in his buttonhole, and putting his lips to a silver goblet of vodka, he would make a speech something like this: 'You are content with my actions, even as I am content with your zeal, whereat I rejoice truly. We are all *brothers*; at our birth we are equal; I drink your health!' He bowed to them, and the peasants bowed to him, but only from the waist, no prostrating themselves to the ground, that was strictly forbidden. The peasants were entertained with good cheer as before, but Ivan Matveitch no longer showed himself to his subjects. Sometimes he interrupted my reading with exclamations: 'La machine se détraque! Cela se gâte!' Even his eyes—those bright, stony eyes—began to grow dim and, as it were, smaller; he dozed oftener than ever and breathed hard in his sleep. His manner with me was unchanged; only a shade of chivalrous deference began to be perceptible in it. He never failed to get up—though with difficulty—from his chair when I came in, conducted me to the door, supporting me with his hand under my elbow, and instead of Suzon began to call me sometimes, 'ma chère demoiselle,' sometimes, 'mon Antigone.' M. le Commandeur died two years after my mother's death; his death seemed to affect Ivan Matveitch far more deeply. A contemporary had disappeared: that was what distressed him. And yet in later years M. le Commandeur's sole service had consisted in crying, 'Bien joué, mal réussi!' every time Ivan Matveitch missed a stroke, playing billiards with Mr. Ratsch; though, indeed, too, when Ivan Matveitch addressed him at table with some such question as: 'N'est-ce pas, M. le Commandeur, c'est Montesquieu qui a dit cela dans ses *Lettres Persanes*?' he had still, sometimes dropping a spoonful of soup on his ruffle, responded profoundly: 'Ah, Monsieur de Montesquieu? Un grand écrivain, monsieur, un grand écrivain!' Only once, when Ivan Matveitch told him that 'les théophilanthropes ont eu pourtant du bon!' the old man cried in an excited voice, 'Monsieur de Kolontouskoi' (he hadn't succeeded in the course of twenty years in learning to pronounce his patron's name correctly), 'Monsieur de Kolontouskoi! Leur fondateur, l'instigateur de cette secte, ce La Reveillère Lepeaux était un bonnet rouge!' 'Non, non,' said Ivan Matveitch, smiling and rolling together a pinch of snuff: 'des fleurs, des jeunes vierges, le culte de la Nature... ils out eu du bon, ils out eu du bon!'...I was always surprised at the extent of Ivan Matveitch's knowledge and at the uselessness of his knowledge to himself.

Ivan Matveitch was perceptibly failing, but he still put a good face on it. One day, three weeks before his death, he had a violent attack of giddiness just after dinner. He sank into thought, said, 'C'est la fin,' and pulling himself together with a sigh, he wrote a letter to Petersburg to his sole heir, a brother with whom he had had no intercourse for twenty years. Hearing that Ivan Matveitch was unwell, a neighbour paid him a visit—a German, a Catholic—once a distinguished physician, who was living in retirement in his little place in the country. He was very rarely at Ivan Matveitch's, but the latter always received him with special deference, and in fact had a great respect for him. He was almost the only person in the world he did respect. The old man advised Ivan Matveitch to send for a priest, but Ivan Matveitch responded that 'ces messieurs et moi, nous n'avons rien à nous dire,' and begged him to change the subject. On the neighbour's departure, he gave his valet orders to admit no one in future.

Then he sent for me. I was frightened when I saw him; there were blue patches under his eyes, his face looked drawn and stiff, his jaw hung down. 'Vous voila grande, Suzon,' he said, with difficulty articulating the consonants, but still trying to smile (I was then nineteen), 'vous allez peut-être bientót rester seule. Soyez toujours sage et vertueuse. C'est la dernière récommandation d'un'—he coughed—'d'un vieillard qui vous veut du bien. Je vous ai recommandé à mon frère et je ne doute pas qu'il ne respecte mes volontés....' He coughed again, and anxiously felt his chest. 'Du reste, j'esèpre encore pouvoir faire quelque chose pour vous... dans mon testament.' This last phrase cut me to the heart, like a knife. Ah, it was really too... too contemptuous and insulting! Ivan Matveitch probably ascribed to some other feeling—to a feeling of grief or gratitude—what was expressed in my face and as though wishing to comfort me, he patted me on the shoulder, at the same time, as usual, gently repelling me, and observed: 'Voyons, mon enfant, du courage! Nous sommes tous mortels! Et puis il n'y a pas encore de danger. Ce n'est qu'une précaution que j'ai cru devoir prendre.... Allez!'

Again, just as when he had summoned me after my mother's death, I longed to shriek at him, 'But I'm your daughter! your daughter!' But I thought in those words, in that cry of the heart, he would doubtless hear nothing but a desire to assert my rights, my claims on his property, on his money.... Oh, no, for nothing in the world would I say a word to this man, who had not once mentioned my mother's name to me, in whose eyes I was of so little account that he did not even trouble himself to ascertain whether I was aware of my parentage! Or, perhaps, he suspected, even knew it, and did not wish 'to raise a dust' (a favourite saying of his, almost the only Russian expression he ever used), did not care to deprive himself of a good reader with a young voice! No! no! Let him go on wronging his daughter, as he had wronged her mother! Let him carry both sins to the grave! I swore it, I swore he should not hear from my lips the word which must have something of a sweet and holy sound in every ear! I would not say to him father! I would not forgive him for my mother and myself! He felt no need of that forgiveness, of that name.... It could not be, it could not be that he felt no need of it! But he should not have forgiveness, he should not, he should not!

God knows whether I should have kept my vow, and whether my heart would not have softened, whether I should not have overcome my shyness, my shame, and my pride... but it happened with Ivan Matveitch just as with my mother. Death carried him off suddenly, and also in the night. It was again Mr. Ratsch who woke me and ran with me to the big house, to Ivan Matveitch's bedroom.... But I found not even the last dying gestures, which had left such a vivid impression on my memory at my mother's bedside. On the embroidered, lace-edged pillows lay a sort of withered, dark-coloured doll, with sharp nose and ruffled grey eyebrows.... I shrieked with horror, with loathing, rushed away, stumbled in doorways against bearded peasants in smocks with holiday red sashes, and found myself, I don't remember how, in the fresh air....

I was told afterwards that when the valet ran into the bedroom, at a violent ring of the bell, he found Ivan Matveitch not in the bed, but a few feet from it. And that he was sitting huddled up on the floor, and that twice over he repeated, 'Well, granny, here's a pretty holiday for you!' And that these were his last words. But I cannot believe that. Was it likely he would speak Russian at such a moment, and such a homely old Russian saying too!

For a whole fortnight afterwards, we were awaiting the arrival of the new master, Semyon Matveitch Koltovsky. He sent orders that nothing was to be touched, no one was to be discharged, till he had looked into everything in person. All the doors, all the furniture, drawers, tables—all were locked and sealed up. All the servants were downcast and apprehensive. I became suddenly one of the most important persons in the house, perhaps the most important. I had been spoken of as 'the young lady' before; but now this expression seemed to take a new significance and was pronounced with a peculiar emphasis. It began to be whispered that 'the old master had died suddenly, and hadn't time to send for a priest, indeed and he hadn't been at confession for many a long day; but still, a will doesn't take long to make.'

Mr. Ratsch, too, thought well to change his mode of action. He did not affect good-nature and friendliness; he knew he would not impose upon me, but his face wore an expression of sulky resignation. 'You see, I give in,' he seemed to say. Everyone showed me deference and tried to please me... while I did not know what to do or how to behave and could only marvel that people failed to perceive how they were hurting me. At last Semyon Matveitch arrived.

Semyon Matveitch was ten years younger than Ivan Matveitch, and his whole life had taken a completely different turn. He was a government official in Petersburg, filling an important position.... He had married and been left early a widower; he had one son. In face Semyon Matveitch was like his brother, only he was shorter and stouter, and had a round bald head, bright black eyes, like Ivan Matveitch's, only more prominent, and full red lips. Unlike his brother, whom he spoke of even after his death as a French philosopher, and sometimes bluntly as a queer fish, Semyon Matveitch almost invariably talked Russian, loudly and fluently, and he was constantly laughing, completely closing his eyes as he did so and shaking all over in an unpleasant way, as though he were shaking with rage. He looked after things very sharply, went into everything himself, and made the strictest account from everyone. The very first day of his arrival he ordered a service with holy water, and sprinkled everything with water, all the rooms in the house, even the lofts and the cellars, in order, as he put it, 'radically to expel the Voltairean and Jacobin spirit.' In the first week several of Ivan Matveitch's favourites were sent to the right-about, one was even banished to a settlement, corporal punishment was inflicted on others; the old valet—he was a Turk, knew French, and had been given to Ivan

Matveitch by the late field-marshal Kamensky—received his freedom, indeed, but with it a command to be gone within twenty-four hours, 'as an example to others.' Semyon Matveitch turned out to be a harsh master; many probably regretted the late owner.

'With the old master, Ivan Matveitch,' a butler, decrepit with age, wailed in my presence, 'our only trouble was to see that the linen put out was clean, and that the rooms smelt sweet, and that the servants' voices weren't heard in the passages—God forbid! For the rest, you might do as you pleased. The old master never hurt a fly in his life! Ah, it's hard times now! It's time to die!'

Rapid, too, was the change in my position, that is to say in the position in which I had been placed for a few days against my own will.... No sort of will was found among Ivan Matveitch's papers, not a line written for my benefit. At once everyone seemed in haste to avoid me.... I am not speaking of Mr. Ratsch... everyone else, too, was angry with me, and tried to show their anger, as though I had deceived them.

One Sunday after matins, in which he invariably officiated at the altar, Semyon Matveitch sent for me. Till that day I had seen him by glimpses, and he seemed not to have noticed me. He received me in his study, standing at the window. He was wearing an official uniform with two stars. I stood still, near the door; my heart was beating violently from fear and from another feeling, vague as yet, but still oppressive. 'I wish to see you, young lady,' began Semyon Matveitch, glancing first at my feet, and then suddenly into my eyes. The look was like a slap in the face. 'I wished to see you to inform you of my decision and to assure you of my unhesitating inclination to be of service to you.' He raised his voice. 'Claims, of course, you have none, but as... my brother's reader you may always reckon on my... my consideration. I am... of course convinced of your good sense and of your principles. Mr. Ratsch, your stepfather, has already received from me the necessary instructions. To which I must add that your attractive exterior seems to me a pledge of the excellence of your sentiments.' Semyon Matveitch went off into a thin chuckle, while I... I was not offended exactly... but I suddenly felt very sorry for myself... and at that moment I fully realised how utterly forsaken and alone I was. Semyon Matveitch went with short, firm steps to the table, took a roll of notes out of the drawer, and putting it in my hand, he added: 'Here is a small sum from me for pocket-money. I won't forget you in future, my pretty; but good-bye for the present, and be a good girl.' I took the roll mechanically: I should have taken anything he had offered me, and going back to my own room, a long while I wept, sitting on my bed. I did not notice that I had dropped the roll of notes on the floor. Mr. Ratsch found it and picked it up, and, asking me what I meant to do with it, kept it for himself.

An important change had taken place in his fortunes too in those days. After a few conversations with Semyon Matveitch, he became a great favourite and soon after received the position of head steward. From that time dates his cheerfulness, that eternal laugh of his; at first it was an effort to adapt himself to his patron... in the end it became a habit. It was then, too, that he became a Russian patriot. Semyon Matveitch was an admirer of everything national, he called himself 'a true Russian bear,' and ridiculed the European dress, which he wore, however. He sent away to a remote village a cook, on whose training Ivan Matveitch had spent vast sums: he sent him away because he had not known how to prepare pickled giblets.

Semyon Matveitch used to stand at the altar and join in the responses with the deacons, and when the serf-girls were brought together to dance and sing choruses, he would join in their songs too, and beat time with his feet, and pinch their cheeks.... But he soon went back to Petersburg, leaving my stepfather practically in complete control of the whole property.

Bitter days began for me.... My one consolation was music, and I gave myself up to it with my whole soul. Fortunately, Mr. Ratsch was very fully occupied, but he took every opportunity to make me feel his hostility; as he had promised, he 'did not forget' my refusal. He ill-treated me, made me copy his long and lying reports to Semyon Matveitch, and correct for him the mistakes in spelling. I was forced to obey him absolutely, and I did obey him. He announced that he meant to tame me, to make me as soft as silk. 'What do you mean by those mutinous eyes?' he shouted sometimes at dinner, drinking his beer, and slapping the table with his hand. 'You think, maybe, you're as silent as a sheep, so you must be all right.... Oh, no! You'll please look at me like a sheep too!' My position became a torture, insufferable,... my heart was growing bitter. Something dangerous began more and more frequently to stir within it. I passed nights without sleep and without a light, thinking, thinking incessantly; and in the darkness without and the gloom within, a fearful determination began to shape itself. The arrival of Semyon Matveitch gave another turn to my thoughts.

No one had expected him. It turned out that he was retiring in unpleasant circumstances; he had hoped to receive the Alexander ribbon, and they had presented him with a snuff-box. Discontented with the government, which had failed to appreciate his talents, and with Petersburg society, which had shown him little sympathy, and did not share his indignation, he determined to settle in the country and devote himself to the management of his property. He arrived alone. His son, Mihail Semyonitch, arrived later, in the holidays for the New Year. My stepfather was scarcely ever out of Semyon Matveitch's room; he still stood high in his good graces. He left me in peace; he had no time for me then... Semyon Matveitch had taken it into his head to start a paper factory. Mr. Ratsch had no knowledge whatever of manufacturing work, and Semyon Matveitch was aware of the fact; but then my stepfather was an active man (the favourite expression just then), an 'Araktcheev!' That was just what Semyon Matveitch used to call him—'my Araktcheev!' 'That's all I want,' Semyon Matveitch maintained; 'if there is zeal, I myself will direct it.' In the midst of his numerous occupations—he had to superintend the factory, the estate, the foundation of a counting-house, the drawing up of counting-house regulations, the creation of new offices and duties—Semyon Matveitch still had time to attend to me.

I was summoned one evening to the drawing-room and set to play the piano. Semyon Matveitch cared for music even less than his brother; he praised and thanked me, however, and next day I was invited to dine at the master's table. After dinner Semyon Matveitch had rather a long conversation with me, asked me questions, laughed at some of my replies, though there was, I remember, nothing amusing in them, and stared at me so strangely... I felt uncomfortable. I did not like his eyes, I did not like their open expression, their clear glance.... It always seemed to me that this very openness concealed something evil, that under that clear brilliance it was dark within in his soul. 'You shall not be my reader,' Semyon Matveitch announced to me at last, prinking and setting himself to rights in a repulsive way. 'I am, thank God, not blind yet, and can read myself; but coffee will taste better to me from your little hands, and I shall listen to your playing with pleasure.' From that day I always went over to the big house to dinner, and sometimes remained in the drawing-room till evening. I too, like my stepfather, was in my favour: it was not a source of joy for me. Semyon Matveitch, I am bound to own, showed me a certain respect, but in the man there was, I felt it, something that repelled and alarmed me. And that 'something' showed itself not in words, but in his eyes, in those wicked eyes, and in his laugh. He never spoke to me of my father, of his brother, and it seemed to me that he avoided the subject, not because he did not want to excite ambitious ideas or pretensions in me, but from another cause, to which I could not give a definite shape, but which made me blush and feel bewildered.... Towards Christmas came his son, Mihail Semyonitch.

Ah, I feel I cannot go on as I have begun; these memories are too painful. Especially now I cannot tell my story calmly.... But what is the use of concealment? I loved Michel, and he loved me.

How it came to pass—I am not going to describe that either. From the very evening when he came into the drawing-room—I was at the piano, playing a sonata of Weber's when he came in—handsome and slender, in a velvet coat lined with sheepskin and high gaiters, just as he was, straight from the frost outside, and shaking his snow-sprinkled, sable cap, before he had greeted his father, glanced swiftly at me, and wondered—I knew that from that evening I could never forget him—I could never forget that good, young face. He began to speak... and his voice went straight to my heart.... A manly and soft voice, and in every sound such a true, honest nature!

Semyon Matveitch was delighted at his son's arrival, embraced him, but at once asked, 'For a fortnight, eh? On leave, eh?' and sent me away.

I sat a long while at my window and gazed at the lights flitting to and fro in the rooms of the big house. I watched them, I listened to the new, unfamiliar voices; I was attracted by the cheerful commotion, and something new, unfamiliar, bright, flitted into my soul too.... The next day before dinner I had my first conversation with him. He had come across to see my stepfather with some message from Semyon Matveitch, and he found me in our little sitting-room. I was getting up to go; he detained me. He was very lively and unconstrained in all his movements and words, but of superciliousness or arrogance, of the tone of Petersburg superiority, there was not a trace in him, and nothing of the officer, of the guardsman.... On the contrary, in the very freedom of his manner there was something appealing, almost shamefaced, as though he were begging you to overlook something. Some people's eyes never laughing, even at the moment of laughter; with *him* it was the lips that almost never changed their beautiful line, while his eyes were almost always smiling. So, we chatted for about an hour... what about I don't remember; I remember only that I looked him straight in the face all the while, and oh, how delightfully at ease I felt with him!

In the evening, I played on the piano. He was very fond of music, and he sat down in a low chair, and laying his curly head on his arm, he listened intently. He did not once praise me, but I felt that he liked my playing, and I played with ardour. Semyon Matveitch, who was sitting near his son, looking through some plans, suddenly frowned. 'Come, madam,' he said, smoothing himself down and buttoning himself up, as his manner was, 'that's enough; why are you trilling away like a canary? It's enough to make one a headache. For us old folks you wouldn't exert yourself so, no fear...' he added in an undertone, and again he sent me away. Michel followed me to the door with his eyes and got up from his seat. 'Where are you off to? Where are you off to?' cried Semyon Matveitch, and he suddenly laughed, and then said something more... I could not catch his words; but Mr. Ratsch, who was present, sitting in a corner of the drawing-room (he was always 'present,' and that time he had brought in the plans), laughed, and his laugh reached my ears.... The same thing, or almost the same thing, was repeated the following evening... Semyon Matveitch grew suddenly cooler to me.

Four days later I met Michel in the corridor that divided the big house in two. He took me by the hand and led me to a room near the dining-room, which was called the portrait gallery. I followed him, not without emotion, but with perfect confidence. Even then, I believe, I would have followed him to the end of the world, though I had as yet no suspicion of all that he was to me. Alas, I loved him with all the passion, all the despair of a young creature who not only has no one to love but feels herself an uninvited and unnecessary guest among strangers, among enemies!... Michel said to me—and it was strange! I looked boldly, directly in his face, while he did not look at me, and flushed slightly—he said to me that he understood my position and sympathised with me and begged me to forgive his father.... 'As far as I'm concerned,' he added, 'I beseech you always to trust me, and believe me, to me you 're a sister—yes, a sister.' Here he pressed my hand warmly. I was confused, it was my turn to look down; I had somehow expected something else; some other word. I began to thank him. 'No, please,'—he cut me short—'don't talk like that.... But remember, it's a brother's duty to defend his sister, and if you ever need protection, against anyone whatever, rely upon me. I have not been here long, but I have seen a good deal already... and among other things, I see through your stepfather.' He squeezed my hand again and left me.

I found out later that Michel had felt an aversion for Mr. Ratsch from his very first meeting with him. Mr. Ratsch tried to ingratiate himself with him too, but becoming convinced of the uselessness of his efforts promptly took up an attitude of hostility to him, and not only did not disguise it from Semyon Matveitch, but, on the contrary, lost no opportunity of showing it, expressing, at the same time, his regret that he had been so unlucky as to displease the young heir. Mr. Ratsch had carefully studied Semyon Matveitch's character; his calculations did not lead him astray. 'This man's devotion to me admits of no doubt, for the very reason that after I am gone he will be ruined; my heir cannot endure him.'...This idea grew and strengthened in the old man's head. They say all persons in power, as they grow old, are readily caught by that bait, the bait of exclusive personal devotion....

Semyon Matveitch had good reason to call Mr. Ratsch his Araktcheev.... He might well have called him another name too. 'You're not one to make difficulties,' he used to say to him. He had begun in this condescendingly familiar tone with him from the very first, and my stepfather would gaze fondly at Semyon Matveitch, let his head droop deprecatingly on one side, and laugh with good-humoured simplicity, as though to say, 'Here I am, entirely in your hands.'

Ah, I feel my hands shaking, and my heart's thumping against the table on which I write at this moment. It's terrible for me to recall those days, and my blood boils.... But I will tell everything to the end... to the end!

A new element had come into Mr. Ratsch's treatment of me during my brief period of favour. He began to be deferential to me, to be respectfully familiar with me, as though I had grown sensible, and become more on a level with him. 'You've done with your airs and graces,' he said to me one day, as we were going back from the big house to the lodge. 'Quite right too! All those fine principles and delicate sentiments—moral precepts in fact—are not for us, young lady, they're not for poor folks.'

When I had fallen out of favour, and Michel did not think it necessary to disguise his contempt for Mr. Ratsch and his sympathy with me, the latter suddenly redoubled his severity with me; he was continually following me about, as though I were capable of any crime, and must be sharply looked after. 'You mind what I say,' he shouted, bursting without knocking into my room, in muddy boots and with his cap on his head; 'I won't put up with such goings on! I won't stand your stuck-up airs! You're not going to impose on me. I'll break your proud spirit.'

And accordingly, one morning he informed me that the decree had gone forth from Semyon Matveitch that I was not to appear at the dinner-table for the future without special invitation.... I don't know how all this would have ended if it had not been for an event which was the final turning-point of my destiny....

Michel was passionately fond of horses. He took it into his head to break in a young horse, which went well for a while, then began kicking and flung him out of the sledge.... He was brought home unconscious, with a broken arm and bruises on his chest. His father was panic-stricken; he sent for the best doctors from the town. They did a great deal for Michel; but he had to lie down for a month. He did not play cards, the doctor forbade him to talk, and it was awkward for him to read, holding the book up in one hand all the while. It ended by Semyon Matveitch sending me into his son, in my old capacity of reader.

Then followed hours I can never forget! I used to go into Michel directly after dinner and sit at a little round table in the half-darkened window. He used to be lying down in a little room out of the drawing-room, at the further end, on a broad leather sofa in the Empire style, with a gold bas-relief on its high, straight back. The bas-relief represented a marriage procession among the ancients. Michel's head, thrown a little back on the pillow, always moved at once, and his pale face turned towards me: he smiled, his whole face brightened, he flung back his soft, damp curls, and said to me softly, 'Good-morning, my kind sweet girl.' I took up the book—Walter Scott's novels were at the height of their fame in those days—the reading of Ivanhoe has left a particularly vivid recollection in my mind.... I could not help my voice thrilling and quivering as I gave utterance to Rebecca's speeches. I, too, had Jewish blood, and was not my lot like hers? Was I not, like Rebecca, waiting on a sick man, dear to me? Every time I removed my eyes from the page and lifted them to him, I met his eyes with the same soft, bright smile over all his face. We talked very little; the door into the drawing-room was invariably open and someone was always sitting there; but whenever it was quiet there, I used, I don't know why, to cease reading and look intently at Michel, and he looked at me, and we both felt happy then and, as it were, glad and shamefaced, and everything, everything we told each other than without a gesture or a word! Alas! our hearts came together, ran to meet each other, as underground streams flow together, unseen, unheard... and irresistibly.

'Can you play chess or draughts?' he asked me one day.

'I can play chess a little,' I answered.

'That's good. Tell them to bring a chess-board and push up the table.'

I sat down beside the sofa, my heart was throbbing, I did not dare glance at Michel,... Yet from the window, across the room, how freely I had gazed at him!

I began to set the chessmen... My fingers shook.

'I suggested it... not for the game,'... Michel said in an undertone, also setting the pieces, 'but to have you nearer me.'

I made no answer, but, without asking which should begin, I moved a pawn... Michel did not move in reply... I looked at him. His head was stretched a little forward; pale all over, with imploring eyes he signed towards my hand...

Whether I understood him... I don't remember, but something instantaneously whirled into my head.... Hesitating, scarcely breathing, I took up the knight and moved it right across the board. Michel bent down swiftly, and catching my fingers with his lips, and pressing them against the board, he began noiselessly and passionately kissing them.... I had no power, I had no wish to draw them back; with my other hand I hid my face, and tears, as I remember now, cold but blissful... oh, what blissful tears!... dropped one by one on the table. Ah, I knew, with my whole heart I felt at that moment, all that he was who held my hand in his power! I knew that he was not a boy, carried away by a momentary impulse, not a Don Juan, not a military Lovelace, but one of the noblest, the best of men... and he loved me!

'Oh, my Susanna!' I heard Michel whisper, 'I will never make you shed other tears than these.'

He was wrong... he did.

But what use is there in dwelling on such memories... especially, especially now?

Michel and I swore to belong to each other. He knew that Semyon Matveitch would never let him marry me, and he did not conceal it from me. I had no doubt about it myself and I rejoiced, not that he did not deceive me—he *could not* deceive—but that he did not try to delude himself. For myself I asked for nothing and would have followed where and how he chose. 'You shall be my wife,' he repeated to me. 'I am not Ivanhoe; I know that happiness is not with Lady Rowena.'

Michel soon regained his health. I could not continue going to see him, but everything was decided between us. I was already entirely absorbed in the future; I saw nothing of what was passing around me, as though I were floating on a glorious, calm, but rushing river, hidden in mist. But we were watched, we were being spied upon. Once or twice, I noticed my stepfather's malignant eyes and heard his loathsome laugh.... But that laugh, those eyes as it had emerged for an instant from the mist... I shuddered, but forgot it directly, and surrendered myself again to the glorious, swift river...

On the day before the departure of Michel—we had planned together that he was to turn back secretly on the way and fetch me—I received from him through his trusted valet a note, in which he asked me to meet him at half-past nine in the summer billiard-room, a large, low-pitched room, built on to the big house in the garden. He wrote to me that he absolutely must speak with me and arrange things. I had twice already met Michel in the billiard-room... I had the key of the outer door. As soon as it struck half-past nine I threw a warm wrap over my shoulders, stepped quietly out of the lodge, and made my way successfully over the crackling snow to the billiard-room. The moon, wrapped in vapour, stood a dim blur just over the ridge of the roof, and the wind whistled shrilly round the corner of the wall. A shiver passed over me, but I put the key into the lock, went into the room, closed the door behind me, turned round... A dark figure became visible against one of the walls, took a couple of steps forward, stopped...

'Michel,' I whispered.

'Michel is locked up by my orders, and this is I!' answered a voice, which seemed to rend my heart...

Before me stood Semyon Matveitch!

I was rushing to escape, but he clutched at my arm.

'Where are you off to, vile hussy?' he hissed. 'You 're quite equal to stolen interviews with young fools, so you'll have to be equal to the consequences.'

I was numb with horror, but still struggled towards the door... In vain! Like iron hooks the ringers of Semyon Matveitch held me tight.

'Let me go, let me go,' I implored at last.

'I tell you....you shan't stir!'

Semyon Matveitch forced me to sit down. In the half-darkness I could not distinguish his face. I had turned away from him too, but I heard him breathing hard and grinding his teeth. I felt neither fear nor despair, but a sort of senseless amazement... A captured bird, I suppose, is numb like that in the claws of the kite... and Semyon Matveitch's hand, which still held me as fast, crushed me like some wild, ferocious claw....

'Aha!' he repeated; 'aha! So, this is how it is... so it's come to this... Ah, wait a bit!'

I tried to get up, but he shook me with such violence that I almost shrieked with pain, and a stream of abuse, insult, and menace burst upon me...

'Michel, Michel, where are you? save me,' I moaned.

Semyon Matveitch shook me again... That time I could not control myself... I screamed.

That seemed to have some effect on him. He became a little quieter, let go my arm, but remained where he was, two steps from me, between me and the door.

A few minutes passed... I did not stir; he breathed heavily as before.

'Sit still,' he began at last, 'and answer me. Let me see that your morals are not yet utterly corrupt, and that you are still capable of listening to the voice of reason. Impulsive folly I can overlook, but stubborn obstinacy—never! My son...' there was a catch in his breath... 'Mihail Semyonitch has promised to marry you? Hasn't he? Answer me! Has he promised, eh?'

I answered, of course, nothing. Semyon Matveitch was almost flying into fury again.

'I take your silence as a sign of assent,' he went on, after a brief pause. 'And so, you were plotting to be my daughter-in-law? A pretty notion! But you're not a child of four years old, and you must be fully aware that young boobies are never sparing of the wildest promises, if only they can gain their ends... but to say nothing of that, could you suppose that I—a noble gentleman of ancient family, Semyon Matveitch Koltovsky—would ever give my consent to such a marriage? Or did you mean to dispense with the parental blessing?... Did you mean to run away, get married in secret and then come back, go through a nice little farce, throw yourself at my feet, in the hope that the old man will be touched.... Answer me, damn you!'

I only bent my head. He could kill me, but to force me to speak—that was not in his power.

He walked up and down a little.

'Come, listen to me,' he began in a calmer voice. 'You mustn't think... don't imagine... I see one must talk to you in a different manner. Listen; I understand your position. You are frightened, upset.... Pull yourself together. At this moment I must seem to you a monster... a despot. But put yourself in my position too; how could I help being indignant, saying too much? And for all that I have shown you that I am not a monster, that I too have a heart. Remember how I treated you on my arrival here and afterwards till... till lately... till the illness of Mihail Semyonitch. I don't wish to boast of my beneficence, but I should have thought simple gratitude ought to have held you back from the slippery path on which you were determined to enter!'

Semyon Matveitch walked to and fro again, and standing still patted me lightly on the arm, on the very arm which still ached from his violence and was marked with blue bruises for long after.

'To be sure,' he began again, 'we're headstrong... just a little headstrong! We don't care to take the trouble to think, we don't care to consider what our advantage consists in and where we ought to seek it. You ask me: where that advantage lies? You've no need to look far.... It's, maybe, close at hand.... Here am I now. As a father, as head of the family I am bound to be particular.... It's my duty. But I'm a man at the same time, and you know that very well. Undoubtedly I'm a practical person and of course cannot tolerate any sentimental nonsense; expectations that are quite inconsistent with everything, you must of course dismiss from your mind for really what sense is there in them?—not to speak of the immorality of such a proceeding.... You will assuredly realise all this yourself, when you have thought it over a little. And I say, simply and straightforwardly, I wouldn't confine myself to what I have done for you. I have always been prepared—and I am still prepared—to put your welfare on a sound footing, to guarantee you a secure position, because I know your value, I do justice to your talents, and your intelligence, and in fact... (here Semyon Matveitch stooped down to me a little)... you have such eyes that, I confess... though I am not a young man, yet to see them quite unmoved... I understand... is not an easy matter, not at all an easy matter.'

These words sent a chill through me. I could scarcely believe my ears. For the first minute I fancied that Semyon Matveitch meant to bribe me to break with Michel, to pay me 'compensation.'... But what was he saying? My eyes had begun to get used to the darkness and I could make out Semyon Matveitch's face. It was smiling, that old face, and he was walking to and fro with little steps, fidgeting restlessly before me....

'Well, what do you say,' he asked at last, 'does my offer please you?'

'Offer?'... I repeated unconsciously,... I simply did not understand a word.

Semyon Matveitch laughed... actually laughed his revolting thin laugh.

'To be sure,' he cried, 'you're all alike you young women'—he corrected himself—'young ladies... young ladies... you all dream of nothing else... you must have young men! You can't live without love! Of course not. Well, well! Youth's all very well! But do you suppose that it's only young men that can love?... There are some older men, whose hearts are warmer... and when once an old man does take a fancy to anyone, well—he's simply like a rock! It's forever! Not like these beardless, feather-brained young fools! Yes, yes; you mustn't look down on old men! They can do so much! You've only got to take them the right way! Yes... yes! And as for kissing, old men know all about that too, he-he-he...' Semyon Matveitch laughed again. 'Come, please... your little hand... just as a proof... that's all....'

I jumped up from the chair, and with all my force I gave him a blow in the chest. He tottered, he uttered a sort of decrepit, scared sound, he almost fell down. There are no words in human language to express how loathsome and infinitely vile he seemed to me. Every vestige of fear had left me.

'Get away, despicable old man,' broke from my lips; 'get away, Mr. Koltovsky, you noble gentleman of ancient family! I, too, am of your blood, the blood of the Koltovskys and I curse the day and the time when I was born of that ancient family!'

'What!... What are you saying!... What!' stammered Semyon Matveitch, gasping for breath. 'You dare... at the very minute when I've caught you... when you came to meet Misha... eh? eh? eh?'

But I could not stop myself.... Something relentless, desperate was roused up within me.

'And you, you, the brother... of your brother, you had the insolence, you dared... What did you take me for? Can you be so blind as not to have seen long ago the loathing you arouse in me?... You dare use the word offer!... Let me out at once, this instant!'

I moved towards the door.

'Oh, indeed! oh, oh! so this is what she says!' Semyon Matveitch piped shrilly, in a fit of violent fury, but obviously not able to make up his mind to come near me.... 'Wait a bit, Mr. Ratsch, Ivan Demianitch, come here!'

The door of the billiard-room opposite the one I was near flew wide open, and my stepfather appeared, with a lighted candelabrum in each hand. His round, red face, lighted up on both sides, was beaming with the triumph of satisfied revenge, and slavish delight at having rendered valuable service.... Oh, those loathsome white eyes! when shall I cease to behold them?

'Be so good as to take this girl at once,' cried Semyon Matveitch, turning to my stepfather and imperiously pointing to me with a shaking hand. 'Be so good as to take her home and put her under lock and key... so that she... can't stir a finger, so that not a fly can get in to her! Till further orders from me! Board up the windows if need be! You'll answer for her with your head!'

Mr. Ratsch set the candelabra on the billiard-table, made Semyon Matveitch a low bow, and with a slight swagger and a malignant smile, moved towards me. A cat, I imagine, approaches a mouse who has no chance of escape in that way. All my daring left me in an instant. I knew the man was capable of... beating me. I began to tremble; yes; oh, shame! oh ignominy! I shivered.

'Now, then, madam,' said Mr. Ratsch, 'kindly come along.'

He took me, without haste, by the arm above the elbow.... He saw that I should not resist. Of my own accord I pushed forward towards the door; at that instant I had but one thought in my mind, to escape as quickly as possible from the presence of Semyon Matveitch.

But the loathsome old man darted up to us from behind, and Ratsch stopped me and turned me round face to face with his patron.

'Ah!' the latter shouted, shaking his fist; 'ah! So, I'm the brother... of my brother, am I? Ties of blood! eh? But a cousin, a first cousin could you marry? Could you? eh? Take her, you!' he turned to my stepfather. 'And remember, keep a sharp look-out! The slightest communication with her—and no punishment will be too severe.... Take her!'

Mr. Ratsch conducted me to my room. Crossing the courtyard, he said nothing, but kept laughing noiselessly to himself. He closed the shutters and the doors, and then, as he was finally returning, he bowed low to me as he had to Semyon Matveitch, and went off into a ponderous, triumphant guffaw!

'Good-night to your highness,' he gasped out, choking: 'she didn't catch her fairy prince! What a pity! It wasn't a bad idea in its way! It's a lesson for the future: not to keep up correspondence! Ho-ho-ho! How capitally it has all turned out though!' He went out, and all of a sudden poked his head in at the door. 'Well? I didn't forget you, did I? Hey? I kept my promise, didn't I? Ho-ho!' The key creaked in the lock. I breathed freely. I had been afraid he would tie my hands... but they were my own, they were free! I instantly wrenched the silken cord off my dressing-gown, made a noose, and was putting it on my neck, but I flung the cord aside again at once. 'I won't please you!' I said aloud. 'What madness, really! Can I dispose of my life without Michel's leave, my life, which I have surrendered into his keeping? No, cruel wretches! No! You have not won your game yet! He will save me, he will tear me out of this hell, he... my Michel!'

But then I remembered that he was shut up just as I was, and I flung myself, face downwards, on my bed, and sobbed... and sobbed.... And only the thought that my tormentor was perhaps at the door, listening and triumphing, only that thought forced me to swallow my tears....

I am worn out. I have been writing since morning, and now it is evening; if once I tear myself from this sheet of paper, I shall not be capable of taking up the pen again.... I must hasten, hasten to the finish! And besides, to dwell on the hideous things that followed that dreadful day is beyond my strength!

Twenty-four hours later I was taken in a closed cart to an isolated hut, surrounded by peasants, who were to watch me, and kept shut up for six whole weeks! I was not for one instant alone.... Later on, I learnt that my stepfather had set spies to watch both Michel and me ever since his arrival, that he had bribed the servant, who had given me Michel's note. I ascertained too that an awful, heart-rending scene had taken place the next morning between the son and the father.... The father had cursed him. Michel for his part had sworn he would never set foot in his father's house again and had set off to Petersburg. But the blow aimed at me by my stepfather rebounded upon himself. Semyon Matveitch announced that he could not have him remaining there and managing the estate any longer. Awkward service, it seems, is an unpardonable offence and someone must be fixed upon to bear the brunt of the *scandal*. Semyon Matveitch recompensed Mr. Ratsch liberally, however: he gave him the necessary means to move to Moscow and to establish himself there. Before the departure for Moscow, I was brought back to the lodge but kept as before under the strictest guard. The loss of the 'snug little berth,' of which he was being deprived 'thanks to me,' increased my stepfather's vindictive rage against me more than ever.

'Why did you make such a fuss?' he would say, almost snorting with indignation; 'upon my word! The old chap, of course, got a little too hot, was a little too much in a hurry, and so he made a mess of it; now, of course, his vanity's hurt, there's no setting the mischief right again now! If you'd only waited a day or two, it'd all have been right as a trivet; you wouldn't have been kept on dry bread, and I should have stayed what I was! Ah, well, women's hair is long... but their wit is short! Never mind; I'll be even with you yet, and that pretty young gentleman shall smart for it too!'

I had, of course, to bear all these insults in silence. Semyon Matveitch I did not once see again. The separation from his son had been a shock to him too. Whether he felt remorse or—which is far more likely—wished to bind me forever to my home, to my family—my family!—anyway, he assigned me a pension, which was to be paid into my stepfather's hands, and to be given to me till I married.... This humiliating alms, this pension I still receive... that is to say, Mr. Ratsch receives it for me....

We settled in Moscow. I swear by the memory of my poor mother, I would not have remained two days, not two hours, with my stepfather, after once reaching the town... I would have gone away, not knowing where... to the police; I would have flung myself at the feet of the governor-general, of the senators; I don't know what I would have done, if it had not happened, at the very moment of our starting from the country, that the girl who had been our maid managed to give me a letter from Michel! Oh, that letter! How many times I read over each line, how many times I covered it with kisses! Michel besought me not to lose heart, to go on hoping, to believe in his unchanging love; he swore that he would never belong to anyone but me; he called me his wife, he promised to overcome all hindrances, he drew a picture of our future, he asked of me only one thing, to be patient, to wait a little....

And I resolved to wait and be patient. Alas! what would I not have agreed to, what would I not have borne, simply to do his will! That letter became my holy thing, my guiding star, my anchor. Sometimes when my stepfather would begin abusing and insulting me, I would softly lay my hand on my bosom (I wore Michel's letter sewed into an amulet) and only smile. And the more violent and abusive was Mr. Ratsch, the easier, lighter, and sweeter was the heart within me.... I used to see, at last, by his eyes, that he began to wonder whether I was going out of my mind.... Following on this first letter came a second, still full of hope.... It spoke of our meeting soon.

Alas! instead of that meeting there came a morning... I can see Mr. Ratsch coming in—and triumph again, malignant triumph, in his face—and in his hands a page of the *Invalid*, and there the announcement of the death of the Captain of the Guards—Mihail Koltovsky.

What can I add? I remained alive and went on living in Mr. Ratsch's house. He hated me as before—more than before—he had unmasked his black soul too much before me, he could not pardon me that. But that was of no consequence to me. I became, as it were, without feeling; my own fate no longer interested me. To think of him, to think of him! I had no interest, no joy, but that. My poor Michel died with my name on his lips.... I was told so by a servant, devoted to him, who had been with him when he came into the country. The same year my stepfather married Eleonora Karpovna. Semyon Matveitch died shortly after. In his will he secured to me and increased the pension he had allowed me.... In the event of my death, it was to pass to Mr. Ratsch....

Two—three—years passed... six years, seven years.... Life has been passing, ebbing away... while I merely watched how it was ebbing. As in childhood, on some river's edge one makes a little pond and dams it up, and tries in all sorts of ways to keep the water from soaking through, from breaking in. But at last, the water breaks in and then you abandon all your vain efforts, and you are glad instead to watch all that you had guarded ebbing away to the last drop....

So, I lived, so I existed, till at last a new, unhoped-for ray of warmth and light....'

The manuscript broke off at this word; the following leaves had been torn off, and several lines completing the sentence had been crossed through and blotted out.

XVIII

The reading of this manuscript so upset me, the impression made by Susanna's visit was so great that I could not sleep all night, and early in the morning I sent an express messenger to Fustov with a letter, in which I besought him to come to Moscow as soon as possible, as his absence might have the most terrible results. I mentioned also my interview with Susanna, and the manuscript she had left in my hands. After having sent off the letter, I did not go out of the house all day and pondered all the time on what might be happening at the Ratsches'. I could not make up my mind to go there myself. I could not help noticing though that my aunt was in a continual fidget; she ordered pastilles to be burnt every minute, and dealt the game of patience, known as 'the traveller,' which is noted as a game in which one can never succeed. The visit of an unknown lady, and at such a late hour, had not been kept secret from her: her imagination at once pictured a yawning abyss on the edge of which I was standing, and she was continually sighing and moaning and murmuring French sentences, quoted from a little manuscript book entitled *Extraits de Lecture*. In the evening, I found on the little table at my bedside the treatise of De Girando, laid open at the chapter: On the evil influence of the passions. This book had been put in my room, at my aunt's instigation of course, by the elder of her companions, who was called in the household Amishka, from her resemblance to a little poodle of that name, and was a very sentimental, not to say romantic, though elderly, maiden lady. All the following day was spent in anxious expectation of Fustov's coming, of a letter from him, of news from the Ratsches' house... though on what ground could they have sent to me? Susanna would be more likely to expect me to visit her.... But I positively could not pluck up courage to see her without first talking to Fustov. I recalled every expression in my letter to him.... I thought it was strong enough; at last, late in the evening, he appeared.

XIX

He came into my room with his habitual, rapid, but deliberate step. His face struck me as pale, and though it showed traces of the fatigue of the journey, there was an expression of astonishment, curiosity, and dissatisfaction—emotions of which he had little experience as a rule. I rushed up to him, embraced him, warmly thanked him for obeying me, and after briefly describing my conversation with Susanna, handed him the manuscript. He went off to the window, to the very window in which Susanna had sat two days before, and without a word to me, he fell to reading it. I at once retired to the opposite corner of the room and for appearance's sake took up a book; but I must own I was stealthily looking over the edge of the cover all the while at Fustov. At first he read rather calmly and kept pulling with his left hand at the bottom on his lip; then he let his hand drop, bent forward and did not stir again. His eyes seemed to fly along the lines and his mouth slightly opened. At last, he finished the manuscript, turned it over, looked round, thought a little and began reading it all through a second time from beginning to end. Then he got up, put the manuscript in his pocket and moved towards the door; but he turned round and stopped in the middle of the room.

'Well, what do you think?' I began, not waiting for him to speak.

'I have acted wrongly towards her,' Fustov declared thickly. 'I have behaved... rashly, unpardonably, cruelly. I believed that... Viktor—'

'What!' I cried; 'that Viktor whom you despise so! But what could he say to you?'

Fustov crossed his arms and stood obliquely to me. He was ashamed, I saw that.

'Do you remember,' he said with some effort, 'that... Viktor alluded to... a pension. That unfortunate word stuck in my head. It's the cause of everything. I began questioning him.... Well and he—'

'What did he say?'

'He told me that the old man... what's his name?... Koltovsky, had allowed Susanna that pension because... on account of... well, in fact, by way of damages.'

I flung up my hands.

'And you believed him?'

Fustov nodded.

'Yes! I believed him.... He said, too, that with the young one... In fact, my behaviour is unjustifiable.'

'And you went away so as to break everything off?'

'Yes; that's the best way... in such cases. I acted savagely, savagely,' he repeated.

We were both silent. Each of us felt that the other was ashamed; but it was easier for me; I was not ashamed of myself.

XX

'I would break every bone in that Viktor's body now,' pursued Fustov, clenching his teeth, 'if I didn't recognise that I'm in fault. I see now what the whole trick was contrived for, with Susanna's marriage they would lose the pension.... Wretches!'

I took his hand.

'Alexander,' I asked him, 'have you been to her?'

'No; I came straight to you on arriving. I'll go tomorrow... early tomorrow. Things can't be left; so, on no account!'

'But you... love her, Alexander?'

Fustov seemed offended.

'Of course I love her. I am very attached to her.'

'She's a splendid, true-hearted girl!' I cried.

Fustov stamped impatiently.

'Well, what notion have you got in your head? I was prepared to marry her—she's been baptized—I'm ready to marry her even now, I'd been thinking of it, though she's older than I am.'

At that instant I suddenly fancied that a pale woman's figure was seated in the window, leaning on her arms. The lights had burnt down; it was dark in the room. I shivered, looked more intently, and saw nothing, of course, in the window seat; but a strange feeling, a mixture of horror, anguish and pity, came over me.

'Alexander!' I began with sudden intensity, 'I beg you; I implore you, go at once to the Ratsches', don't put it off till tomorrow! An inner voice tells me that you really ought to see Susanna today!'

Fustov shrugged his shoulders.

'What are you talking about, really! It's eleven o'clock now, most likely they're all in bed.'

'No matter.... Do go, for goodness' sake! I have a presentiment.... Please do as I say! Go at once, take a sledge....'

'Come, what nonsense!' Fustov responded coolly; 'how could I go now? Tomorrow morning, I will be there, and everything will be cleared up.'

'But, Alexander, remember, she said that she was dying, that you would not find her... And if you had seen her face! Only think, imagine, to make up her mind to come to me... what it must have cost her....'

'She's a little high-flown,' observed Fustov, who had apparently regained his self-possession completely. 'All girls are like that... at first. I repeat, everything will be all right tomorrow. Meanwhile, good-bye. I'm tired, and you're sleepy too.'

He took his cap and went out of the room.

'But you promise to come here at once, and tell me all about it?' I called after him.

'I promise.... Good-bye!'

I went to bed, but in my heart I was uneasy, and I felt vexed with my friend. I fell asleep late and dreamed that I was wandering with Susanna along the underground, damp passages of some sort, and crawling along narrow, steep staircases, and continually going deeper and deeper down, though we were trying to get higher up out into the air. Someone was calling us all the while incessantly in monotonous, plaintive tones.

XXI

Some one's hand lay on my shoulder and pushed it several times.... I opened my eyes and in the faint light of the solitary candle, I saw Fustov standing before me. He frightened me. He was staggering; his face was yellow, almost the same colour as his hair; his lips seemed hanging down, his muddy eyes were staring senselessly away. What had become of his invariably amiable, sympathetic expression? I had a cousin who from epilepsy was sinking into idiocy.... Fustov looked like him at that moment.

I sat up hurriedly.

'What is it? What is the matter? Heavens!'

He made no answer.

'Why, what has happened? Fustov! Do speak! Susanna?...'

Fustov gave a slight start.

'She...' he began in a hoarse voice and broke off.

'What of her? Have you seen her?'

He stared at me.

'She's no more.'

'No more?'

'No. She is dead.'

I jumped out of bed.

'Dead? Susanna? Dead?'

Fustov turned his eyes away again.

'Yes; she is dead; she died at midnight.'

'He's raving!' crossed my mind.

'At midnight! And what's the time now?'

'It's eight o'clock in the morning now.

They sent me to tell. She is to be buried tomorrow.'

I seized him by the hand.

'Alexander, you're not delirious? Are you in your senses?'

'I am in my senses,' he answered. 'Directly I heard it, I came straight to you.'

My heart turned sick and numb, as always happens on realising an irrevocable misfortune.

'My God! my God! Dead!' I repeated. 'How is it possible? So suddenly! Or perhaps she took her own life?'

'I don't know,' said Fustov, 'I know nothing. They told me she died at midnight. And tomorrow she will be buried.'

'At midnight!' I thought ... 'Then she was still alive yesterday when I fancied I saw her in the window, when I entreated him to hasten to her....'

'She was still alive yesterday, when you wanted to send me to Ivan Demianitch's,' said Fustov, as though guessing my thought.

'How little he knew her!' I thought again. 'How little we both knew her! "High-flown," he said, "all girls are like that."... And at that very minute, perhaps, she was putting to her lips... Can one love anyone and be so grossly mistaken in them?'

Fustov stood stock-still before my bed, his hands hanging, like a guilty man.

XXII

I dressed hurriedly.

'What do you mean to do now, Alexander?' I asked.

He gazed at me in bewilderment, as though marvelling at the absurdity of my question. And indeed, what was there to do?

'You simply must go to them, though,' I began. 'You're bound to ascertain how it happened; there is, possibly, a crime concealed. One may expect anything of those people.... It is all to be thoroughly investigated. Remember the statement in her manuscript, the pension was to cease on her marriage, but in event of her death it was to pass to Ratsch. In any case, one must render her the last duty, pay homage to her remains!'

I talked to Fustov like a preceptor, like an elder brother. In the midst of all that horror, grief, bewilderment, a sort of unconscious feeling of superiority over Fustov had suddenly come to the surface in me.... Whether from seeing him crushed by the consciousness of his fault, distracted, shattered, whether that a misfortune befalling a man almost always humiliates him, lowers him in the opinion of others, 'you can't be much,' is felt, 'if you hadn't the wit to come off better than that!' God knows! Anyway, Fustov seemed to me almost like a child, and I felt pity for him, and saw the necessity of severity. I held out a helping hand to him, stooping down to him from above. Only a woman's sympathy is free from condescension.

But Fustov continued to gaze with wild and stupid eyes at me—my authoritative tone obviously had no effect on him, and to my second question, 'You're going to them, I suppose?' he replied—

'No, I'm not going.'

'What do you mean, really? Don't you want to ascertain for yourself, to investigate, how, and what? Perhaps, she has left a letter... a document of some sort....'

Fustov shook his head.

'I can't go there,' he said. 'That's what I came to you for, to ask you to go... for me... I can't... I can't....'

Fustov suddenly sat down to the table, hid his face in both hands, and sobbed bitterly.

'Alas, alas!' he kept repeating through his tears; 'alas, poor girl... poor girl... I loved... I loved her... alas!'

I stood near him, and I am bound to confess, not the slightest sympathy was excited in me by those incontestably sincere sobs. I simply marvelled that Fustov could cry like that, and it seemed to me that now I knew what a small person he was, and that I should, in his place, have acted quite differently. What's one to make of it? If Fustov had remained quite unmoved, I should perhaps have hated him, have conceived an aversion for him, but he would not have sunk in my esteem.... He would have kept his prestige. Don Juan would have remained Don Juan! Very late in life, and only after many experiences, does a man learn, at the sight of a fellow-creature's real failing or weakness, to sympathise with him and help him without a secret self-congratulation at his own virtue and strength, but on the contrary, with every humility and comprehension of the naturalness, almost the inevitableness, of sin.

XXIII

I was very bold and resolute in sending Fustov to the Ratsches'; but when I set out there myself at twelve o'clock (nothing would induce Fustov to go with me, he only begged me to give him an exact account of everything), when round the corner of the street their house glared at me in the distance with a yellowish blur from the coffin candles at one of the windows, an indescribable panic made me hold my breath, and I would gladly have turned back.... I mastered myself, however, and went into the passage. It smelt of incense and wax; the pink cover of the coffin, edged with silver lace, stood in a corner, leaning against the wall. In one of the adjoining rooms, the dining-room, the monotonous muttering of the deacon droned like the buzzing of a bee. From the drawing-room peeped out the sleepy face of a servant girl, who murmured in a subdued voice, 'Come to do homage to the dead?' She indicated the door of the dining-room. I went in. The coffin stood with the head towards the door; the black hair of Susanna under the white wreath, above the raised lace of the pillow, first caught my eyes.

I went up sidewards, crossed myself, bowed down to the ground, glanced... Merciful God! what a face of agony! Unhappy girl! even death had no pity on her, had denied her—beauty, that would be little—even that peace, that tender and impressive peace which is often seen on the faces of the newly dead. The little, dark, almost brown, face of Susanna recalled the visages on old, old holy pictures. And the expression on that face! It looked as though she were on the point of shrieking—a shriek of despair—and had died so, uttering no sound... even the line between the brows was not smoothed out, and the fingers on the hands were bent back and clenched. I turned away my eyes involuntarily; but, after a brief interval, I forced myself to look, to look long and attentively at her. Pity filled my soul, and not pity alone. 'That girl died by violence,' I decided inwardly; 'that's beyond doubt.' While I was standing looking at the dead girl, the deacon, who on my entrance had raised his voice and uttered a few disconnected sounds, relapsed into droning again, and yawned twice. I bowed to the ground a second time and went out into the passage.

In the doorway of the drawing-room Mr. Ratsch was already on the look-out for me, dressed in a gay-coloured dressing-gown. Beckoning to me with his hand, he led me to his own room—I had almost said to his lair. The room, dark and close, soaked through and through with the sour smell of stale tobacco, suggested a comparison with the lair of a wolf or a fox.

XXIV

'Rupture! rupture of the external... of the external covering.... You understand.., the envelopes of the heart!' said Mr. Ratsch, directly closing the door. 'Such a misfortune! Only yesterday evening there was nothing to notice, and all of a sudden, all in a minute, all was over! It's a true saying, "heute roth, morgen todt!" It's true; it's what was to be expected. I always expected it. At Tambov the regimental doctor, Galimbovsky, Vikenty Kasimirovitch.... you've probably heard of him... a first-rate medical man, a specialist—'

'It's the first time I've heard the name,' I observed.

'Well, no matter; any way he was always,' pursued Mr. Ratsch, at first in a low voice, and then louder and louder, and, to my surprise, with a perceptible German accent, 'he was always warning me: "Ay, Ivan Demianitch! ay! my dear boy, you must be careful! Your stepdaughter has an organic defect in the heart—hypertrophia cordialis! The last thing and there'll be trouble! She must avoid all exciting emotions above all.... You must appeal to her reason."... But, upon my word, with a young lady... can one appeal to reason? Ha... ha... ha...'

Mr. Ratsch was, through long habit, on the point of laughing, but he recollected himself in time and changed the incipient guffaw into a cough.

And this was what Mr. Ratsch said! After all that I had found out about him!... I thought it my duty, however, to ask him whether a doctor was called in.

Mr. Ratsch positively bounced into the air.

'To be sure there was.... Two were summoned, but it was already over—abgemacht! And only fancy, both, as though they were agreeing' (Mr. Ratsch probably meant, as though they had agreed), 'rupture! rupture of the heart! That's what, with one voice, they cried out. They proposed a post-mortem; but I... you understand, did not consent to that.'

'And the funeral's tomorrow?' I queried.

'Yes, yes, tomorrow, tomorrow we bury our dear one! The procession will leave the house precisely at eleven o'clock in the morning.... From here to the church of St. Nicholas on Hen's Legs... what strange names your Russian churches do have, you know! Then to the last resting-place in mother earth. You will come! We have not been long acquainted, but I make bold to say, the amiability of your character and the elevation of your sentiments!...'

I made haste to nod my head.

'Yes, yes, yes,' sighed Mr. Ratsch. 'It... it really has been, as they say, a thunderbolt from a clear sky! Ein Blitz aus heiterem Himmel!'

'And Susanna Ivanovna said nothing before her death, left nothing?'

'Nothing, positively! Not a scrap of anything! Not a bit of paper! Only fancy, when they called me to her, when they woke me up—she was stiff already! It was very distressing for me; she has grieved us all terribly! Alexander Daviditch will be sorry too, I dare say, when he knows.... They say he is not in Moscow.'

'He did leave town for a few days...' I began.

'Viktor Ivanovitch is complaining they're so long getting his sledge harnessed,' interrupted a servant girl coming in—the same girl I had seen in the passage. Her face, still looking half-awake, struck me this time by the expression of coarse insolence to be seen in servants when they know that their masters are in their power, and that they do not dare to find fault or be exacting with them.

'Directly, directly,' Ivan Demianitch responded nervously. 'Eleonora Karpovna! Leonora! Lenchen! come here!'

There was a sound of something ponderous moving the other side of the door, and at the same instant I heard Viktor's imperious call: 'Why on earth don't they put the horses in? You don't catch me trudging off to the police on foot!'

'Directly, directly,' Ivan Demianitch faltered again. 'Eleonora Karpovna, come here!'

'But, Ivan Demianitch,' I heard her voice, 'ich habe keine Toilette gemacht!'

'Macht nichts. Komm herein!'

Eleonora Karpovna came in, holding a kerchief over her neck with two fingers. She had on a morning wrapper, not buttoned up, and had not yet done her hair. Ivan Demianitch flew up to her.

'You hear, Viktor's calling for the horses,' he said, hurriedly pointing his finger first to the door, then to the window. 'Please, do see to it, as quick as possible! Der Kerl schreit so!'

'Der Viktor schreit immer, Ivan Demianitch, Sie wissen wohl,' responded Eleonora Karpovna, 'and I have spoken to the coachman myself, but he's taken it into his head to give the horses oats. Fancy, what a calamity to happen so suddenly,' she added, turning to me; 'who could have expected such a thing of Susanna Ivanovna?'

'I was always expecting it, always!' cried Ratsch, and threw up his arms, his dressing-gown flying up in front as he did so, and displaying most repulsive unmentionables of chamois leather, with buckles on the belt.

'Rupture of the heart! rupture of the external membrane! Hypertrophy!'

'To be sure,' Eleonora Karpovna repeated after him, 'hyper... Well, so it is. Only it's a terrible, terrible grief to me, I say again...' And her coarse-featured face worked a little, her eyebrows rose into the shape of triangles, and a tiny tear rolled over her round cheek, that looked varnished like a doll's.... 'I'm very sorry that such a young person who ought to have lived and enjoyed everything... everything... And to fall into despair so suddenly!'

'Na! gut, gut... geh, alte!' Mr. Ratsch cut her short.

'Geh' schon, geh' schon,' muttered Eleonora Karpovna, and she went away, still holding the kerchief with her fingers, and shedding tears.

And I followed her. In the passage stood Viktor in a student's coat with a beaver collar and a cap stuck jauntily on one side. He barely glanced at me over his shoulder, shook his collar up, and did not nod to me, for which I mentally thanked him.

I went back to Fustov.

XXV

I found my friend sitting in a corner of his room with a downcast head and arms folded across his breast. He had sunk into a state of numbness, and he gazed around him with the slow, bewildered look of a man who has slept very heavily and has only just been waked. I told him all about my visit to Ratsch's, repeated the veteran's remarks and those of his wife, described the impression they had made on me and informed him of my conviction that the unhappy girl had taken her own life.... Fustov listened to me with no change of expression and looked about him with the same bewildered air.

'Did you see her?' he asked me at last.

'Yes.'

'In the coffin?'

Fustov seemed to doubt whether Susanna were really dead.

'In the coffin.'

Fustov's face twitched and he dropped his eyes and softly rubbed his hands.

'Are you cold?' I asked him.

'Yes, old man, I'm cold,' he answered hesitatingly, and he shook his head stupidly.

I began to explain my reasons for thinking that Susanna had poisoned herself or perhaps had been poisoned, and that the matter could not be left so....

Fustov stared at me.

'Why, what is there to be done?' he said, slowly opening his eyes wide and slowly closing them. 'Why, it'll be worse... if it's known about. They won't bury her. We must let things... alone.'

This idea, simple as it was, had never entered my head. My friend's practical sense had not deserted him.

'When is... her funeral?' he went on.

'Tomorrow.'

'Are you going?'

'Yes.'

'To the house or straight to the church?'

'To the house and to the church too; and from there to the cemetery.'

'But I shan't go... I can't, I can't!' whispered Fustov and began crying. It was at these same words that he had broken into sobs in the morning. I have noticed that it is often so with weeping; as though to certain words, for the most of no great meaning,—but just to these words and to no others—it is given to open the fount of tears in a man, to break him down, and to excite in him the feeling of pity for others and himself... I remember a peasant woman was once describing before me the sudden death of her daughter, and she fairly dissolved and could not go on with her tale as soon as she uttered the phrase, 'I said to her, Fekla. And she says, "Mother, where have you put the salt... the salt... sa-alt?"' The word 'salt' overpowered her.

But again, as in the morning, I was but little moved by Fustov's tears. I could not conceive how it was he did not ask me if Susanna had not left something for him. Altogether their love for one another was a riddle to me; and a riddle remained to me.

After weeping for ten minutes Fustov got up, lay down on the sofa, turned his face to the wall, and remained motionless. I waited a little, but seeing that he did not stir, and made no answer to my questions, I made up my mind to leave him. I am perhaps doing him injustice, but I almost believe he was asleep. Though indeed that would be no proof that he did not feel sorrow... only his nature was so constituted as to be unable to support painful emotions for long... His nature was too awfully well-balanced!

XXVI

The next day exactly at eleven o'clock I was at the place. Fine hail was falling from the low-hanging sky, there was a slight frost, a thaw was close at hand, but there were cutting, disagreeable gusts of wind flitting across in the air.... It was the most thoroughly Lenten, cold-catching weather. I found Mr. Ratsch on the steps of his house. In a black frock-coat adorned with crape, with no hat on his head, he fussed about, waved his arms, smote himself on the thighs, shouted up to the house, and then down into the street, in the direction of the funeral car with a white catafalque, already standing there with two hired carriages. Near it four garrison soldiers, with mourning capes over their old coats, and mourning hats pulled over their screwed-up eyes, were pensively scratching in the crumbling snow with the long stems of their unlighted torches. The grey shock of hair positively stood up straight above the red face of Mr. Ratsch, and his voice, that brazen voice, was cracking from the strain he was putting on it. 'Where are the pine branches? pine branches! this way! the branches of pine!' he yelled. 'They'll be bearing out the coffin directly! The pine! Hand over those pine branches! Look alive!' he cried once more and dashed into the house. It appeared that in spite of my punctuality, I was late: Mr. Ratsch had thought fit to hurry things forward. The service in the house was already over; the priests—of whom one wore a calotte, and the other, rather younger, had most carefully combed and oiled his hair—appeared with all their retinue on the steps. The coffin too appeared soon after, carried by a coachman, two door-keepers, and a water-carrier. Mr. Ratsch walked behind, with the tips of his fingers on the coffin lid, continually repeating, 'Easy, easy!' Behind him waddled Eleonora Karpovna in a black dress, also adorned with crape, surrounded by her whole family; after all of them, Viktor stepped out in a new uniform with a sword with crape round the handle. The coffin-bearers, grumbling and altercating among themselves, laid the coffin on the hearse; the garrison soldiers lighted their torches, which at once began crackling and smoking; a stray old woman, who had joined herself on to the party, raised a wail; the deacons began to chant, the fine snow suddenly fell faster and whirled round like 'white flies.' Mr. Ratsch bawled, 'In God's name! start!' and the procession started. Besides Mr. Ratsch's family, there were in all five men accompanying the hearse: a retired and extremely shabby officer of roads and highways, with a faded Stanislas ribbon—not improbably hired—on his neck; the police superintendent's assistant, a diminutive man with a meek face and greedy eyes; a little old man in a fustian smock; an extremely fat fishmonger in a tradesman's bluejacket, smelling strongly of his calling, and I. The absence of the female sex (for one could hardly count as such two aunts of Eleonora Karpovna, sisters of the sausage maker, and a hunchback old maiden lady with blue spectacles on her blue nose), the absence of girl friends and acquaintances struck me at first; but on thinking it over I realised that Susanna, with her character, her education, her memories, could not have made friends in the circle in which she was living. In the church there were a good many people assembled, more outsiders than acquaintances, as one could see by the expression of their faces. The service did not last long. What surprised me was that Mr. Ratsch crossed himself with great fervour, quite as though he were of the orthodox faith, and even chimed in with the deacons in the responses, though only with the notes not with the words. When at last it came to taking leave of the dead, I bowed low, but did not give the last kiss. Mr. Ratsch, on the contrary, went through this terrible ordeal with the utmost composure, and with a deferential inclination of his person invited the officer of the Stanislas ribbon to the coffin, as though offering him entertainment, and picking his children up under the arms swung them up in turn and held them up to the body. Eleonora Karpovna, on taking farewell of Susanna, suddenly broke into a roar that filled the church; but she was soon soothed and continually asked in an exasperated whisper, 'But where's my reticule?' Viktor held himself aloof and seemed to be trying by his whole demeanour to convey that he was out of sympathy with all such customs and was only performing a social duty. The person who showed the most sympathy was the little old man in the smock, who had been, fifteen years before, a land surveyor in the Tambov province, and had not seen Ratsch since then. He did not know Susanna at all but had drunk a couple of glasses of spirits at the sideboard before starting. My aunt had also come to the church. She had somehow or other found out that the deceased woman was the very lady who had paid me a visit and had been thrown into a state of indescribable agitation! She could not bring herself to suspect me of any sort of misconduct, but neither could she explain such a strange chain of circumstances.... Not improbably she imagined that Susanna had been led by love for me to commit suicide, and attired in her darkest garments, with an aching heart and tears, she prayed on her knees for the peace of the soul of the departed and put a rouble candle before the picture of the Consolation of Sorrow.... 'Amishka' had come with her too, and she too prayed, but was for the most part gazing at me, horror-stricken.... That elderly spinster, alas! did not regard me with indifference. On leaving the church, my aunt distributed all her money, more than ten roubles, among the poor.

At last, the farewell was over. They began closing the coffin. During the whole service I had not courage to look straight at the poor girl's distorted face; but every time that my eyes passed by it—'he did not come, he did not come,' it seemed to me that it wanted to say. They were just going to lower the lid upon the coffin. I could not restrain myself: I turned a rapid glance on to the dead woman. 'Why did you do it?' I was unconsciously asking.... 'He did not come!' I fancied for the last time.... The hammer was knocking in the nails, and all was over.

XXVII

We followed the hearse towards the cemetery. We were forty in number, of all sorts and conditions, nothing else really than an idle crowd. The wearisome journey lasted more than an hour. The weather became worse and worse. Halfway there Viktor got into a carriage, but Mr. Ratsch stepped gallantly on through the sloppy snow; just so must he have stepped through the snow when, after the fateful interview with Semyon Matveitch, he led home with him in triumph the girl whose life he had ruined forever. The 'veteran's' hair and eyebrows were edged with snow; he kept blowing and uttering exclamations, or manfully drawing deep breaths and puffing out his round, dark-red cheeks.... One really might have thought he was laughing. 'On my death the pension was to pass to Ivan Demianitch'; these words from Susanna's manuscript recurred again to my mind. We reached the cemetery at last; we moved up to a freshly dug grave. The last ceremony was quickly performed; all were chilled through; all were in haste. The coffin slid on cords into the yawning hole; they began to throw earth on it. Mr. Ratsch here too showed the energy of his spirit, so rapidly, with such force and vigour, did he fling clods of earth on to the coffin lid, throwing himself into a heroic pose, with one leg planted firmly before him... he could not have shown more energy if he had been stoning his bitterest foe. Viktor, as before, held himself aloof; he kept muffling himself up in his coat, and rubbing his chin in the fur of his collar. Mr. Ratsch's other children eagerly imitated their father. Flinging sand and earth was a source of great enjoyment to them, for which, of course, they were in no way to blame. A mound began to rise up where the hole had been; we were on the point of separating, when Mr. Ratsch, wheeling round to the left in soldierly fashion, and slapping himself on the thigh, announced to all of us 'gentlemen present,' that he invited us, and also the 'reverend clergy,' to a 'funeral banquet,' which had been arranged at no great distance from the cemetery, in the chief saloon of an extremely superior restaurant, 'thanks to the kind offices of our honoured friend Sigismund Sigismundovitch.'... At these words he indicated the assistant of the police superintendent and added that for all his grief and his Lutheran faith, he, Ivan Demianitch Ratsch, as a genuine Russian, put the old Russian usages before everything. 'My spouse,' he cried, 'with the ladies that have accompanied her, may go home, while we gentlemen commemorate in a modest repast the shade of Thy departed servant!' Mr. Ratsch's proposal was received with genuine sympathy; 'the reverend clergy' exchanged expressive glances with one another, while the officer of roads and highways slapped Ivan Demianitch on the shoulder and called him a patriot and the soul of the company.

We set off all together to the restaurant. In the restaurant, in the middle of a long, wide, and quite empty room on the first storey, stood two tables laid for dinner, covered with bottles and eatables, and surrounded by chairs. The smell of whitewash, mingled with the odours of spirits and salad oil, was stifling and oppressive. The police superintendent's assistant, as the organiser of the banquet, placed the clergy in the seats of honour, near which the Lenten dishes were crowded together conspicuously; after the priests the other guests took their seats; the banquet began. I would not have used such a festive word as banquet by choice, but no other word would have corresponded with the real character of the thing. At first the proceedings were fairly quiet, even slightly mournful; jaws munched busily, and glasses were emptied, but sighs too were audible—possibly sighs of digestion, but possibly also of feeling. There were references to death, allusions to the brevity of human life, and the fleeting nature of earthly hopes. The officer of roads and highways related a military but still edifying anecdote. The priest in the calotte expressed his approval, and himself contributed an interesting fact from the life of the saint, Ivan the Warrior. The priest with the superbly arranged hair, though his attention was chiefly engrossed by the edibles, gave utterance to something improving on the subject of chastity. But little by little all this changed. Faces grew redder, and voices grew louder, and laughter reasserted itself; one began to hear disconnected exclamations, caressing appellations, after the manner of 'dear old boy,' 'dear heart alive,' 'old cock,' and even 'a pig like that'—everything, in fact, of which the Russian nature is so lavish, when, as they say, 'it comes unbuttoned.' By the time that the corks of home-made champagne were popping, the party had become noisy; someone even crowed like a cock, while another guest was offering to bite up and swallow the glass out of which he had just been drinking. Mr. Ratsch, no longer red but purple, suddenly rose from his seat; he had been guffawing and making a great noise before, but now he asked leave to make a speech. 'Speak! Out with it!' everyone roared; the old man in the smock even bawled 'bravo!' and clapped his hands... but he was already sitting on the floor. Mr. Ratsch lifted his glass high above his head and announced that he proposed in brief but 'impressionable' phrases to refer to the qualities of the noble soul which,' leaving here, so to say, its earthly husk (die irdische Hülle) has soared to heaven, and plunged...' Mr. Ratsch corrected himself: 'and plashed....' He again corrected himself: 'and plunged...'

'Father deacon! Reverend sir! My good soul!' we heard a subdued but insistent whisper, 'they say you've a devilish good voice; honour us with a song, strike up: "We live among the fields!"'

'Sh! sh!... Shut up there!' passed over the lips of the guests.

...'Plunged all her devoted family,' pursued Mr. Ratsch, turning a severe glance in the direction of the lover of music, 'plunged all her family into the most irreplaceable grief! Yes!' cried Ivan Demianitch, 'well may the Russian proverb say, "Fate spares not the rod."...'

'Stop! Gentlemen!' shouted a hoarse voice at the end of the table, 'my purse has just been stolen!...'

'Ah, the swindler!' piped another voice, and slap! went a box on the ear.

Heavens! What followed then! It was as though the wild beast, till then only growling and faintly stirring within us, had suddenly broken from its chains and reared up, ruffled and fierce in all its hideousness. It seemed as though everyone had been secretly expecting 'a scandal,' as the natural outcome and sequel of a banquet, and all, as it were, rushed to welcome it, to support it.... Plates, glasses clattered and rolled about, chairs were upset, a deafening din arose, hands were waving in the air, coat-tails were flying, and a fight began in earnest.

'Give it him! give it him!' roared like mad my neighbour, the fishmonger, who had till that instant seemed to be the most peaceable person in the world; it is true he had been silently drinking some dozen glasses of spirits. 'Thrash him!...'

Who was to be thrashed, and what he was to be thrashed for, he had no idea, but he bellowed furiously.

The police superintendent's assistant, the officer of roads and highways, and Mr. Ratsch, who had probably not expected such speedy termination to his eloquence, tried to restore order... but their efforts were unavailing. My neighbour, the fishmonger, even fell afoul of Mr. Ratsch himself.

'He's murdered the young woman, the blasted German,' he yelled at him, shaking his fists; 'he's bought over the police, and here he's crowing over it!!'

At this point the waiters ran in.... What happened further I don't know; I snatched up my cap in all haste, and made off as fast as my legs would carry me! All I remember is a fearful crash; I recall, too, the remains of a herring in the hair of the old man in the smock, a priest's hat flying right across the room, the pale face of Viktor huddled up in a corner, and a red beard in the grasp of a muscular hand.... Such were the last impressions I carried away of the 'memorial banquet,' arranged by the excellent Sigismund Sigismundovitch in honour of poor Susanna.

After resting a little, I set off to see Fustov and told him all of which I had been a witness during that day. He listened to me, sitting still, and not raising his head, and putting both hands under his legs, he murmured again, 'Ah! my poor girl, my poor girl!' and again lay down on the sofa and turned his back on me.

A week later he seemed to have quite got over it and took up his life as before. I asked him for Susanna's manuscript as a keepsake: he gave it me without raising any objection.

XXVIII

Several years passed by. My aunt was dead; I had left Moscow and settled in Petersburg. Fustov too had moved to Petersburg. He had entered the department of the Ministry of Finance, but we rarely met, and I saw nothing much in him then. An official like everyone else, and nothing more! If he is still living and not married, he is, most likely, unchanged to this day; he carves and carpenters and uses dumb-bells, and is as much a lady-killer as ever, and sketches Napoleon in a blue uniform in the albums of his lady friends. It happened that I had to go to Moscow on business. In Moscow I learned, with considerable surprise, that the fortunes of my former acquaintance, Mr. Ratsch, had taken an adverse turn. His wife had, indeed, presented him with twins, two boys, whom as a true Russian he had christened Briacheslav and

Viacheslav, but his house had been burnt down, he had been forced to retire from his position, and worst of all, his eldest son, Viktor, had become practically a permanent inmate of the debtors' prison. During my stay in Moscow, among a company at a friendly gathering, I chanced to hear an allusion made to Susanna, and a most slighting, most insulting allusion! I did all I could to defend the memory of the unhappy girl, to whom fate had denied even the charity of oblivion, but my arguments did not make much impression on my audience. One of them, a young student poet, was, however, a little moved by my words. He sent me next day a poem, which I have forgotten, but which ended in the following four lines:

'Her tomb lies cold, forlorn, but even death
Her gentle spirit's memory cannot save
From the sly voice of slander whispering on,
Withering the flowers on her forsaken tomb....'

I read these lines and unconsciously sank into musing. Susanna's image rose before me; once more I seemed to see the frozen window in my room; I recalled that evening and the blustering snowstorm, and those words, those sobs.... I began to ponder how it was possible to explain Susanna's love for Fustov, and why she had so quickly, so impulsively given way to despair, as soon as she saw herself forsaken. How was it she had had no desire to wait a little, to hear the bitter truth from the lips of the man she loved, to write to him, even? How could she fling herself at once headlong into the abyss? Because she was passionately in love with Fustov, I shall be told; because she could not bear the slightest doubt of his devotion, of his respect for her. Perhaps, or perhaps because she was not at all so passionately in love with Fustov; that she did not deceive herself about him, but simply rested her last hopes on him, and could not get over the thought that even this man had at once, at the first breath of slander, turned away from her with contempt! Who can say what killed her; wounded pride, or the wretchedness of her helpless position, or the very memory of that first, noble, true-hearted nature to whom she had so joyfully pledged herself in the morning of her early days, who had so deeply trusted her, and so honoured her? Who knows; perhaps at the very instant when I fancied that her dead lips were murmuring, 'he did not come!' her soul was rejoicing that she had gone herself to him, to her Michel? The secrets of human life are great, and love itself, the most impenetrable of those secrets.... Anyway, to this day, whenever the image of Susanna rises before me, I cannot overcome a feeling of pity for her, and of angry reproach against fate and my lips whisper instinctively, 'Unhappy girl! unhappy girl!'

1868.

THE JEW

'Tell us a story, colonel,' we said at last to Nikolai Ilyitch.

The colonel smiled, puffed out a coil of tobacco smoke between his moustaches, passed his hand over his grey hair, looked at us and considered. We all had the greatest liking and respect for Nikolai Ilyitch, for his good-heartedness, common sense, and kindly indulgence to us young fellows. He was a tall, broad-shouldered, stoutly-built man; his dark face, 'one of the splendid Russian faces,' *[Footnote: Lermontov in the Treasurer's Wife.—AUTHOR'S NOTE.] straight-forward, clever glance, gentle smile, manly and mellow voice—everything about him pleased and attracted one.*

'All right, listen then,' he began.

It happened in 1813, before Dantzig. I was then in the E—— regiment of cuirassiers, and had just, I recollect, been promoted to be a cornet. It is an exhilarating occupation—fighting; and marching too is good enough in its way, but it is fearfully slow in a besieging army. There one sits the whole blessed day within some sort of entrenchment, under a tent, on mud or straw, playing cards from morning till night. Perhaps, from simple boredom, one goes out to watch the bombs and red-hot bullets flying.

At first the French kept us amused with sorties, but they quickly subsided. We soon got sick of foraging expeditions too; we were overcome, in fact, by such deadly dullness that we were ready to howl for sheer *ennui*. I was not more than nineteen then; I was a healthy young fellow, fresh as a daisy, thought of nothing but getting all the fun I could out of the French... and in other ways too... you understand what I mean... and this is what happened. Having nothing to do, I fell to gambling. All of a sudden, after dreadful losses, my luck turned, and towards morning (we used to play at night) I had won an immense amount. Exhausted and sleepy, I came out into the fresh air and sat down on a mound. It was a splendid, calm morning; the long lines of our fortifications were lost in the mist; I gazed till I was weary, and then began to doze where I was sitting.

A discreet cough waked me: I opened my eyes, and saw standing before me a Jew, a man of forty, wearing a long-skirted grey wrapper, slippers, and a black smoking-cap. This Jew, whose name was Girshel was continually hanging about our camp, offering his services as an agent, getting us wine, provisions and other such trifles. He was a thinnish, red-haired, little man, marked with smallpox; he blinked incessantly with his diminutive, little eyes, which were reddish too; he had a long-crooked nose and was always coughing.

He began fidgeting about me, bowing obsequiously.

'Well, what do you want?' I asked him at last.

'Oh, I only—I've only come, sir, to know if I can't be of use to your honour in some way...'

'I don't want you; you can go.'

'At your honour's service, as you desire.... I thought there might be, sir, something....'

'You bother me; go along, I tell you.'

'Certainly, sir, certainly. But your honour must permit me to congratulate you on your success....'

'Why, how did you know?'

'Oh, I know, to be sure I do.... An immense sum... immense....Oh! how immense....'

Girshel spread out his fingers and wagged his head.

'But what's the use of talking,' I said peevishly; 'what the devil's the good of money here?'

'Oh! don't say that your honour; ay, ay, don't say so. Money's a capital thing; always of use; you can get anything for money, your honour; anything! anything! Only say the word to the agent, he'll get you anything, your honour anything! anything!'

'Don't tell lies, Jew.'

'Ay! ay!' repeated Girshel, shaking his side-locks. 'Your honour doesn't believe me.... Ay... ay....' The Jew closed his eyes and slowly wagged his head to right and to left.... 'Oh, I know what his honour the officer would like.... I know,... to be sure I do!'

The Jew assumed an exceedingly knowing leer.

'Really!'

The Jew glanced round timorously, then bent over to me.

'Such a lovely creature, your honour, lovely!...' Girshel again closed his eyes and shot out his lips.

'Your honour, you've only to say the word... you shall see for yourself... whatever I say now, you'll hear... but you won't believe... better tell me to show you... that's the thing, that's the thing!'

I did not speak; I gazed at the Jew.

'Well, all right then; well then, very good; so, I'll show you then....'

Thereupon Girshel laughed and slapped me lightly on the shoulder but skipped back at once as though he had been scalded.

'But, your honour, how about a trifle in advance?'

'But you're taking me in, and will show me some scarecrow?'

'Ay, ay, what a thing to say!' the Jew pronounced with unusual warmth, waving his hands about. 'How can you! Why... if so, your honour, you order me to be given five hundred... four hundred and fifty lashes,' he added hurriedly....'You give orders—'

At that moment one of my comrades lifted the edge of his tent and called me by name. I got up hurriedly and flung the Jew a gold coin.

'This evening, this evening,' he muttered after me.

I must confess, my friends, I looked forward to the evening with some impatience. That very day the French made a sortie; our regiment marched to the attack. The evening came on; we sat round the fires... the soldier's cooked porridge. My comrades talked. I lay on my cloak, drank tea, and listened to my comrades' stories. They suggested a game of cards—I refused to take part in it. I felt excited. Gradually the officers dispersed to their tents; the fires began to die down; the soldiers too dispersed or went to sleep on the spot; everything was still. I did not get up. My orderly squatted on his heels before the fire and was beginning to nod. I sent him away. Soon the whole camp was hushed. The sentries were relieved. I still lay there, as if it were waiting for something. The stars peeped out. The night came on. A long while I watched the dying flame.... The last fire went out. 'The damned Jew was taking me in,' I thought angrily, and was just going to get up.

'Your honour,'... a trembling voice whispered close to my ear.

I looked round: Girshel. He was very pale, he stammered and whispered something.

'Let's go to your tent, sir.' I got up and followed him. The Jew shrank into himself, and stepped warily over the short, damp grass. I observed on one side a motionless, muffled-up figure. The Jew beckoned to her—she went up to him. He whispered to her, turned to me, nodded his head several times and we all three went into the tent. Ridiculous to relate, I was breathless.

'You see, your honour,' the Jew whispered with an effort, 'you see. She's a little frightened at the moment, she's frightened; but I've told her his honour the officer's a good man, a splendid man.... Don't be frightened, don't be frightened,' he went on—'don't be frightened....'

The muffled-up figure did not stir. I was myself in a state of dreadful confusion, and didn't know what to say. Girshel too was fidgeting restlessly and gesticulating in a strange way....

'Any way,' I said to him, 'you get out....' Unwillingly, as it seemed, Girshel obeyed.

I went up to the muffled-up figure, and gently took the dark hood off her head. There was a conflagration in Dantzig: by the faint, reddish, flickering glow of the distant fire I saw the pale face of a young Jewess. Her beauty astounded me. I stood facing her and gazed at her in silence. She did not raise her eyes. A slight rustle made me look round. Girshel was cautiously poking his head in under the edge of the tent. I waved my hand at him angrily,... he vanished.

'What's your name?' I said at last.

'Sara,' she answered, and for one instant I caught in the darkness the gleam of the whites of her large, long-shaped eyes and little, even, flashing teeth.

I snatched up two leather cushions, flung them on the ground, and asked her to sit down. She slipped off her shawl and sat down. She was wearing a short Cossack jacket, open in front, with round, chased silver buttons, and full sleeves. Her thick black hair was coiled twice round her little head. I sat down beside her and took her dark, slender hand. She resisted a little, but seemed afraid to look at me, and there was a catch in her breath. I admired her Oriental profile and timidly pressed her cold, shaking fingers.

'Do you know Russian?'

'Yes... a little.'

'And do you like Russians?'

'Yes, I like them.'

'Then, you like me too?'

'Yes, I like you.'

I tried to put my arm round her, but she moved away quickly....

'No, no, please, sir, please...'

'Oh, all right; look at me, anyway.'

She let her black, piercing eyes rest upon me, and at once turned away with a smile, and blushed.

I kissed her hand ardently. She peeped at me from under her eyelids and softly laughed.

'What is it?'

She hid her face in her sleeve and laughed more than before.

Girshel showed himself at the entrance of the tent and shook his finger at her. She ceased laughing.

'Go away!' I whispered to him through my teeth; 'you make me sick!'

Girshel did not go away.

I took a handful of gold pieces out of my trunk, stuffed them in his hand and pushed him out.

'Your honour, me too....' she said.

I dropped several gold coins on her lap; she pounced on them like a cat.

'Well, now I must have a kiss.'

'No, please, please,' she faltered in a frightened and beseeching voice.

'What are you frightened of?'

'I'm afraid.'

'Oh, nonsense....'

'No, please.'

She looked timidly at me, put her head a little on one side and clasped her hands. I let her alone.

'If you like... here,' she said after a brief silence, and she raised her hand to my lips. With no great eagerness, I kissed it. Sara laughed again.

My blood was boiling. I was annoyed with myself and did not know what to do. Really, I thought at last, what a fool I am.

I turned to her again.

'Sara, listen, I'm in love with you.'

'I know.'

'You know? And you're not angry? And do you like me too?'

Sara shook her head.

'No, answer me properly.'

'Well, show yourself,' she said.

I bent down to her. Sara laid her hands on my shoulders, began scrutinising my face, frowned, smiled.... I could not contain myself and gave her a rapid kiss on her cheek. She jumped up and in one bound was at the entrance of the tent.

'Come, what a shy thing you are!'

She did not speak and did not stir.

'Come here to me....'

'No, sir, good-bye. Another time.'

Girshel again thrust in his curly head and said a couple of words to her; she bent down and glided away, like a snake.

I ran out of the tent in pursuit of her but could not get another glimpse of her or of Girshel.

The whole night long I could not sleep a wink.

The next night we were sitting in the tent of our captain; I was playing, but with no great zest. My orderly came in.

'Some one's asking for you, your honour.'

'Who is it?'

'A Jew.'

'Can it be Girshel?' I wondered. I waited till the end of the rubber, got up and went out. Yes, it was so; I saw Girshel.

'Well,' he questioned me with an ingratiating smile, 'your honour, are you satisfied?'

'Ah, you———!' (Here the colonel glanced round. 'No ladies present, I believe.... Well, never mind, anyway.') 'Ah, bless you!' I responded, 'so you're making fun of me, are you?'

'How so?'

'How so, indeed! What a question!'

'Ay, ay, your honour, you 're too bad,' Girshel said reproachfully, but never ceasing smiling. 'The girl is young and modest.... You frightened her; indeed, you did.'

'Queer sort of modesty! why did she take money, then?'

'Why, what then? If one's given money, why not take it, sir?'

'I say, Girshel, let her come again, and I'll let you off... only, please, don't show your stupid phiz inside my tent, and leave us in peace; do you hear?'

Girshel's eyes sparkled.

'What do you say? You like her?'

'Well, yes.'

'She's a lovely creature! there's not another such anywhere. And have you something for me now?'

'Yes, here, only listen; fair play is better than gold. Bring her and then go to the devil. I'll escort her home myself.'

'Oh, no, sir, no, that's impossible, sir,' the Jew rejoined hurriedly. 'Ay, ay, that's impossible. I'll walk about near the tent, your honour, if you like; I'll... I'll go away, your honour, if you like, a little.... I'm ready to do your honour a service.... I'll move away... to be sure, I will.'

'Well, mind you do.... And bring her, do you hear?'

'Eh, but she's a beauty, your honour, eh? your honour, a beauty, eh?'

Girshel bent down and peeped into my eyes.

'She's good-looking.'

'Well, then, give me another gold piece.'

I threw him a coin; we parted.

The day passed at last. The night came on. I had been sitting for a long while alone in my tent. It was dark outside. It struck two in the town. I was beginning to curse the Jew.... Suddenly Sara came in, alone. I jumped up took her in my arms... put my lips to her face.... It was cold as ice. I could scarcely distinguish her features.... I made her sit down, knelt down before her, took her hands, touched her waist.... She did not speak, did not stir, and suddenly she broke into loud, convulsive sobbing. I tried in vain to soothe her, to persuade her.... She wept in torrents.... I caressed her, wiped her tears; as before, she did not resist, made no answer to my questions and wept—wept, like a waterfall. I felt a pang at my heart; I got up and went out of the tent.

Girshel seemed to pop up out of the earth before me.

'Girshel,' I said to him, 'here's the money I promised you. Take Sara away.'

The Jew at once rushed up to her. She left off weeping, and clutched hold of him.

'Good-bye, Sara,' I said to her. 'God bless you, good-bye. We'll see each other again some other time.'

Girshel was silent and bowed humbly. Sara bent down, took my hand and pressed it to her lips; I turned away....

For five or six days, my friends, I kept thinking of my Jewess. Girshel did not make his appearance, and no one had seen him in the camp. I slept rather badly at nights; I was continually haunted by wet, black eyes, and long eyelashes; my lips could not forget the touch of her cheek, smooth and fresh as a downy plum. I was sent out with a foraging party to a village some distance away. While my soldiers were ransacking the houses, I remained in the street, and did not dismount from my horse. Suddenly someone caught hold of my foot....

'Mercy on us, Sara!'

She was pale and excited.

'Your honour... help us, save us, your soldiers are insulting us.... Your honour....'

She recognised me and flushed red.

'Why, do you live here?'

'Yes.'

'Where?'

Sara pointed to a little, old house. I set spurs to my horse and galloped up. In the yard of the little house an ugly and tattered Jewess was trying to tear out of the hands of my long sergeant, Siliavka, three hens and a duck. He was holding his booty above his head, laughing; the hens clucked, and the duck quacked.... Two other cuirassiers were loading their horses with hay, straw, and sacks of flour. Inside the house I heard shouts and oaths in Little-Russian.... I called to my men and told them to leave the Jews alone, not to take anything from them. The soldiers obeyed, the sergeant got on his grey mare, Proserpina, or, as he called her, 'Prozherpila,' and rode after me into the street.

'Well,' I said to Sara, 'are you pleased with me?'

She looked at me with a smile.

'What has become of you all this time?'

She dropped her eyes.

'I will come to you tomorrow.'

'In the evening?'

'No, sir, in the morning.'

'Mind you do, don't deceive me.'

'No... no, I won't.'

I looked greedily at her. By daylight she seemed to me more handsome than ever. I remember I was particularly struck by the even, amber tint of her face and the bluish lights in her black hair.... I bent down from my horse and warmly pressed her little hand.

'Good-bye, Sara... mind you come.'

'Yes.'

She went home; I told the sergeant to follow me with the party and galloped off.

The next day I got up very early, dressed, and went out of the tent. It was a glorious morning; the sun had just risen, and every blade of grass was sparkling in the dew and the crimson glow. I clambered on to a high breastwork and sat down on the edge of an embrasure. Below me a stout, cast-iron cannon stuck out its black muzzle towards the open country. I looked carelessly about me... and all at once caught sight of a bent figure in a grey wrapper, a hundred paces from me. I recognised Girshel. He stood without moving for a long while in one place, then suddenly ran a little on one side, looked hurriedly and furtively round... uttered a cry, squatted down, cautiously craned his neck and began looking round again and listening. I could see all his actions very clearly. He put his hand into his bosom, took out a scrap of paper and a pencil, and began writing or drawing something. Girshel continually stopped, started like a hare, attentively scrutinised everything around him, and seemed to be sketching our camp. More than once, he hid his scrap of paper, half closed his eyes, sniffed at the air, and again set to work. At last, the Jew squatted down on the grass, took off his slipper, and stuffed the paper in it; but he had not time to regain his legs, when suddenly, ten steps from him, there appeared from behind the slope of an earthwork the whiskered countenance of the sergeant Siliavka, and gradually the whole of his long clumsy figure rose up from the ground. The Jew stood with his back to him. Siliavka went quickly up to him and laid his heavy paw on his shoulder. Girshel seemed to shrink into himself. He shook like a leaf and uttered a feeble cry, like a hare's. Siliavka addressed him threateningly and seized him by the collar. I could not hear their conversation, but from the despairing gestures of the Jew, and his supplicating appearance, I began to guess what it was. The Jew twice flung himself at the sergeant's feet, put his hand in his pocket, pulled out a torn check handkerchief, untied a knot, and took out gold coins.... Siliavka took his offering with great dignity, but did not leave off dragging the Jew by the collar. Girshel made a sudden bound and rushed away; the sergeant sped after him in pursuit. The Jew ran exceedingly well; his legs, clad in blue stockings, flashed by, really very rapidly; but Siliavka after a short run caught the crouching Jew, made him stand up, and carried him in his arms straight to the camp. I got up and went to meet him.

'Ah! your honour!' bawled Siliavka,—'it's a spy I'm bringing you—a spy!...' The sturdy Little-Russian was streaming with perspiration. 'Stop that wriggling, devilish Jew—now then... you wretch! you'd better look out, I'll throttle you!'

The luckless Girshel was feebly prodding his elbows into Siliavka's chest and feebly kicking.... His eyes were rolling convulsively....

'What's the matter?' I questioned Siliavka.

'If your honour'll be so good as to take the slipper off his right foot,—I can't get at it.' He was still holding the Jew in his arms.

I took off the slipper, took out of it a carefully folded piece of paper, unfolded it, and found an accurate map of our camp. On the margin were a number of notes written in a fine hand in the Jews' language.

Meanwhile Siliavka had set Girshel on his legs. The Jew opened his eyes, saw me, and flung himself on his knees before me.

Without speaking, I showed him the paper.

'What's this?'

'It's—-nothing, your honour. I was only....' His voice broke.

'Are you a spy?'

He did not understand me, muttered disconnected words, pressed my knees in terror....

'Are you a spy?'

'I!' he cried faintly and shook his head. 'How could I? I never did; I'm not at all. It's not possible; utterly impossible. I'm ready—I'll—this minute—I've money to give... I'll pay for it,' he whispered, and closed his eyes.

The smoking-cap had slipped back on to his neck; his reddish hair was soaked with cold sweat, and hung in tails; his lips were blue, and working convulsively; his brows were contracted painfully; his face was drawn....

Soldiers came up round us. I had at first meant to give Girshel a good fright, and to tell Siliavka to hold his tongue, but now the affair had become public, and could not escape 'the cognisance of the authorities.'

'Take him to the general,' I said to the sergeant.

'Your honour, your honour!' the Jew shrieked in a voice of despair. 'I am not guilty... not guilty.... Tell him to let me go, tell him...'

'His Excellency will decide about that,' said Siliavka. 'Come along.'

'Your honour!' the Jew shrieked after me—'tell him! have mercy!'

His shriek tortured me; I hastened my pace. Our general was a man of German extraction, honest and good-hearted, but strict in his adherence to military discipline. I went into the little house that had been hastily put up for him, and in a few words explained the reason of my visit. I knew the severity of the military regulations, and so I did not even pronounce the word 'spy,' but tried to put the whole affair before him as something quite trifling and not worthwhile. But, unhappily for Girshel, the general put doing his duty higher than pity.

'You, young man,' he said to me in his broken Russian, 'inexperienced are. You are in military matters yet inexperienced. The matter, of which you to me reported have, is important, very important.... And where is this man who taken was? this Jew? where is he?'

I went out and told them to bring in the Jew. They brought in the Jew. The wretched creature could scarcely stand up.

'Yes,' pronounced the general, turning to me; 'and where's the plan which on this man found was?'

I handed him the paper. The general opened it, turned away again, screwed up his eyes, frowned....

'This is most as-ton-ish-ing...' he said slowly. 'Who arrested him?'

'I, your Excellency!' Siliavka jerked out sharply.

'Ah! good! good!... Well, my good man, what do you say in your defence?'

'Your... your... your Excellency,' stammered Girshel, 'I... indeed,... your Excellency... I'm not guilty... your Excellency; ask his honour the officer.... I'm an agent, your Excellency, an honest agent.'

'He ought to be cross-examined,' the general murmured in an undertone, wagging his head gravely. 'Come, how do you explain this, my friend?' 'I'm not guilty, your Excellency, I'm not guilty.'

'That is not probable, however. You were—how is it said in Russian?—taken on the fact, that is, in the very facts!'

'Hear me, your Excellency; I am not guilty.'

'You drew the plan? you are a spy of the enemy?'

'It wasn't me!' Girshel shrieked suddenly; 'not I, your Excellency!'

The general looked at Siliavka.

'Why, he's raving, your Excellency. His honour the officer here took the plan out of his slipper.'

The general looked at me. I was obliged to nod assent.

'You are a spy from the enemy, my good man....'

'Not I... not I...' whispered the distracted Jew.

'You have the enemy with similar information before provided? Confess....'

'How could I?'

'You will not deceive me, my good man. Are you a spy?'

The Jew closed his eyes, shook his head, and lifted the skirts of his gown.

'Hang him,' the general pronounced expressively after a brief silence,' according to the law. Where is Mr. Fiodor Schliekelmann?'

They ran to fetch Schliekelmann, the general's adjutant. Girshel began to turn greenish, his mouth fell open, his eyes seemed starting out of his head. The adjutant came in. The general gave him the requisite instructions. The secretary showed his sickly, pock-marked face for an instant. Two or three officers peeped into the room inquisitively.

'Have pity, your Excellency,' I said to the general in German as best I could; 'let him off....'

'You, young man,' he answered me in Russian, 'I was saying to you, are inexperienced, and therefore I beg you silent to be, and me no more to trouble.'

Girshel with a shriek dropped at the general's feet.

'Your Excellency, have mercy; I will never again, I will not, your Excellency; I have a wife... your Excellency, a daughter... have mercy....'

'It's no use!'

'Truly, your Excellency, I am guilty... it's the first time, your Excellency, the first time, believe me!'

'You furnished no other documents?'

'The first time, your Excellency,... my wife... my children... have mercy....'

'But you are a spy.'

'My wife... your Excellency... my children....'

The general felt a twinge, but there was no getting out of it.

'According to the law, hang the Hebrew,' he said constrainedly, with the air of a man forced to do violence to his heart, and sacrifice his better feelings to inexorable duty—'hang him! Fiodor Karlitch, I beg you to draw up a report of the occurrence....'

A horrible change suddenly came over Girshel. Instead of the ordinary timorous alarm peculiar to the Jewish nature, in his face was reflected the horrible agony that comes before death. He writhed like a wild beast trapped, his mouth stood open, there was a hoarse rattle in his throat, he positively leapt up and down, convulsively moving his elbows. He had on only one slipper; they had forgotten to put the other on again... his gown fell open... his cap had fallen off....

We all shuddered; the general stopped speaking.

'Your Excellency,' I began again, 'pardon this wretched creature.'

'Impossible! It is the law,' the general replied abruptly, and not without emotion, 'for a warning to others.'

'For pity's sake....'

'Mr. Cornet, be so good as to return to your post,' said the general, and he motioned me imperiously to the door.

I bowed and went out. But seeing that in reality I had no post anywhere, I remained at no great distance from the general's house.

Two minutes later Girshel made his appearance, conducted by Siliavka and three soldiers. The poor Jew was in a state of stupefaction and could hardly move his legs. Siliavka went by me to the camp, and soon returned with a rope in his hands. His coarse but not ill-natured face wore a look of strange, exasperated commiseration. At the sight of the rope the Jew flung up his arms, sat down, and burst into sobs. The soldiers stood silently about him and stared grimly at the earth. I went up to Girshel, addressed him; he sobbed like a baby, and did not even look at me. With a hopeless gesture I went to my tent, flung myself on a rug, and closed my eyes....

Suddenly someone ran hastily and noisily into my tent. I raised my head and saw Sara; she looked beside herself. She rushed up to me and clutched at my hands.

'Come along, come along,' she insisted breathlessly.

'Where? what for? let us stop here.'

''To father, to father, quick... save him... save him!'

'To what father?'

'My father; they are going to hang him....'

'What! is Girshel...?'

'My father... I'll tell you all about it later,' she added, wringing her hands in despair: 'only come... come....'

We ran out of the tent. In the open ground, on the way to a solitary birch-tree, we could see a group of soldiers.... Sara pointed to them without speaking....

'Stop,' I said to her suddenly: 'where are we running to? The soldiers won't obey me.'

Sara still pulled me after her.... I must confess, my head was going round.

'But listen, Sara,' I said to her; 'what sense is there in running here? It would be better for me to go to the general again; let's go together; who knows, we may persuade him.'

Sara suddenly stood still and gazed at me, as though she were crazy.

'Understand me, Sara, for God's sake. I can't do anything for your father, but the general can. Let's go to him.'

'But meanwhile they'll hang him,' she moaned....

I looked round. The secretary was standing not far off.

'Ivanov,' I called to him; 'run, please, over there to them, tell them to wait a little, say I've gone to petition the general.'

'Yes, sir.'

Ivanov ran off.

We were not admitted to the general's presence. In vain, I begged, persuaded, swore even at last... in vain, poor Sara tore her hair and rushed at the sentinels; they would not let us pass.

Sara looked wildly round, clutched her head in both hands, and ran at breakneck pace towards the open country, to her father. I followed her. Everyone stared at us, wondering.

We ran up to the soldiers. They were standing in a ring, and picture it, gentlemen! they were laughing, laughing at poor Girshel. I flew into a rage and shouted at them. The Jew saw us and fell on his daughter's neck. Sara clung to him passionately.

The poor wretch imagined he was pardoned.... He was just beginning to thank me... I turned away.

'Your honour,' he shrieked and wrung his hands; 'I'm not pardoned?'

I did not speak.

'No?'

'No.'

'Your honour,' he began muttering; 'look, your honour, look... she, this girl, see—you know—she's my daughter.'

'I know,' I answered, and turned away again.

'Your honour,' he shrieked, 'I never went away from the tent! I wouldn't for anything...'

He stopped and closed his eyes for an instant.... 'I wanted your money, your honour, I must own... but not for anything....'

I was silent. Girshel was loathsome to me, and she too, his accomplice....

'But now, if you save me,' the Jew articulated in a whisper, 'I'll command her... I... do you understand?... everything... I'll go to every length....'

He was trembling like a leaf and looking about him hurriedly. Sara silently and passionately embraced him.

The adjutant came up to us.

'Cornet,' he said to me; 'his Excellency has given me orders to place you under arrest. And you...' he motioned the soldiers to the Jew... 'quickly.'

Siliavka went up to the Jew.

'Fiodor Karlitch,' I said to the adjutant (five soldiers had come with him); 'tell them, at least, to take away that poor girl....'

'Of course. Certainly.'

The unhappy girl was scarcely conscious. Girshel was muttering something to her in Yiddish....

The soldiers with difficulty freed Sara from her father's arms, and carefully carried her twenty steps away. But all at once she broke from their arms and rushed towards Girshel.... Siliavka stopped her. Sara pushed him away; her face was covered with a faint flush, her eyes flashed, she stretched out her arms.

'So may you be accursed,' she screamed in German; 'accursed, thrice accursed, you and all the hateful breed of you, with the curse of Dathan and Abiram, the curse of poverty and sterility and violent, shameful death! May the earth open under your feet, godless, pitiless, bloodthirsty dogs....'

Her head dropped back... she fell to the ground.... They lifted her up and carried her away.

The soldiers took Girshel under his arms. I saw then why it was they had been laughing at the Jew when I ran up from the camp with Sara. He was really ludicrous, in spite of all the horror of his position. The intense anguish of parting with life, his daughter, his family, showed itself in the Jew in such strange and grotesque gesticulations, shrieks, and wriggles that we all could not help smiling, though it was horrible—intensely horrible to us too. The poor wretch was half dead with terror....

'Oy! oy! oy!' he shrieked: 'oy... wait! I've something to tell you... a lot to tell you. Mr. Under-sergeant, you know me. I'm an agent, an honest agent. Don't hold me; wait a minute, a little minute, a tiny minute—wait! Let me go; I'm a poor Hebrew. Sara... where is Sara? Oh, I know, she's at his honour the quarter-lieutenant's.' (God knows why he bestowed such an unheard-of grade upon me.) 'Your honour the quarter-lieutenant, I'm not going away from the tent.' (The soldiers were taking hold of Girshel... he uttered a deafening shriek and wriggled out of their hands.) 'Your Excellency, have pity on the unhappy father of a family. I'll give you ten golden pieces, fifteen I'll give, your Excellency!...' (They dragged him to the birch-tree.) 'Spare me! have mercy! your honour the quarter-lieutenant! your Excellency, the general and commander-in-chief!'

They put the noose on the Jew.... I shut my eyes and rushed away.

I remained for a fortnight under arrest. I was told that the widow of the luckless Girshel came to fetch away the clothes of the deceased. The general ordered a hundred roubles to be given to her. Sara I never saw again. I was wounded, I was taken to the hospital, and by the time I was well again, Dantzig had surrendered, and I joined my regiment on the banks of the Rhine.

THREE PORTRAITS

'Neighbours' constitute one of the most serious drawbacks of life in the country. I knew a country gentleman of the Vologodsky district, who used on every suitable occasion to repeat the following words, 'Thank God, I have no neighbours,' and I confess I could not help envying that happy mortal. My own little place is situated in one of the most thickly peopled provinces of Russia. I am surrounded by a vast number of dear neighbours, from highly respectable and highly respected country gentlemen, attired in ample frockcoats and still more ample waistcoats, down to regular loafers, wearing jackets with long sleeves and a so-called shooting-bag on their back. In this crowd of gentlefolks I chanced, however, to discover one very pleasant fellow. He had served in the army, had retired and settled for good and all in the country. According to his story, he had served for two years in the B——— regiment. But I am totally unable to comprehend how that man could have performed any sort of duty, not merely for two years, but even for two days. He was born 'for a life of peace and country calm,' that is to say, for lazy, careless vegetation, which, I note parenthetically, is not without great and inexhaustible charms. He possessed a very fair property, and without giving too much thought to its management, spent about ten thousand roubles a year, had obtained an excellent cook—my friend was fond of good fare—and ordered too from Moscow all the newest French books and magazines. In Russian he read nothing but the reports of his bailiff, and that with great difficulty. He used, when he did not go out shooting, to wear a dressing-gown from morning till dinner-time and at dinner. He would look through plans of some sort or go round to the stables or to the threshing barn, and joke with the peasant women, who, to be sure, in his presence wielded their flails in leisurely fashion. After dinner my friend would dress very carefully before the looking-glass and drive off to see some neighbour possessed of two or three pretty daughters. He would flirt serenely and unconcernedly with one of them, play blind-man's-buff with them, return home rather late and promptly fall into a heroic sleep. He could never be bored, for he never gave himself up to complete inactivity; and in the choice of occupations, he was not difficult to please and was amused like a child with the smallest trifle. On the other hand, he cherished no particular attachment to life, and at times, when he chanced to get a glimpse of the track of a wolf or a fox, he would let his horse go at full gallop over such ravines that to this day I cannot understand how it was he did not break his neck a hundred times over. He belonged to that class of persons who inspire in one the idea that they do not know their own value, that under their appearance of indifference strong and violent passions lie concealed. But he would have laughed in one's face if he could have guessed that one cherished such an opinion of him. And indeed, I must own I believe myself that even supposing my friend had had in youth some strong impulse, however vague, towards what is so sweetly called 'higher things,' that impulse had long, long ago died out. He was rather stout and enjoyed superb health. In our day one cannot help liking people who think little about themselves, because they are exceedingly rare... and my friend had almost forgotten his own personality. I fancy, though, that I have said too much about him already, and my prolixity is the more uncalled for as he is not the hero of my story. His name was Piotr Fedorovitch Lutchinov.

One autumn day there were five of us, ardent sportsmen, gathered together at Piotr Fedorovitch's. We had spent the whole morning out, had run down a couple of foxes and a number of hares and had returned home in that supremely agreeable frame of mind which comes over every well-regulated person after a successful day's shooting. It grew dusk. The wind was frolicking over the dark fields and noisily swinging the bare tops of the birches and lime-trees round Lutchinov's house. We reached the house, got off our horses.... On the steps I stood still and looked round: long storm-clouds were creeping heavily over the grey sky; a dark-brown bush was writhing in the wind and murmuring plaintively; the yellow grass helplessly and forlornly bowed down to the earth; flocks of thrushes were fluttering in the mountain-ashes among the bright, flame-coloured clusters of berries. Among the light brittle twigs of the birch-trees blue-tits hopped whistling. In the village there was the hoarse barking of dogs. I felt melancholy... but it was with a genuine sense of comfort that I walked into the dining-room. The shutters were closed; on a round table, covered with a tablecloth of dazzling whiteness, amid cut-glass decanters of red wine, there were eight lighted candles in silver candlesticks; a fire glowed cheerfully on the hearth, and an old and very stately-looking butler, with a huge bald head, wearing an English dress, stood before another table on which was pleasingly conspicuous a large soup-tureen, encircled by light savoury-smelling steam. In the hall we passed by another venerable man, engaged in icing champagne—'according to the strictest rules of the art.' The dinner was, as is usual in such cases, exceedingly pleasant. We laughed and talked of the incidents of the day's shooting, and recalled with enthusiasm two glorious 'runs.' After dining pretty heartily, we settled comfortably into ample arm-chairs round the fire; a huge silver bowl made its appearance on the table, and in a few minutes the white flame of the burning rum announced our host's agreeable intention 'to concoct a punch.' Piotr Fedoritch was a man of some taste; he was aware, for instance, that nothing has so fatal an influence on the fancy as the cold, steady, pedantic light of a lamp, and so he gave orders that only two candles should be left in the room. Strange half-shadows quivered on the walls, thrown by the fanciful play of the fire in the hearth and the flame of the punch... a soft, exceedingly agreeable sense of soothing comfort replaced in our hearts the somewhat boisterous gaiety that had reigned at dinner.

Conversations have their destinies, like books, as the Latin proverb says, like everything in the world. Our conversation that evening was particularly many-sided and lively. From details it passed to rather serious general questions, and lightly and casually came back to the daily incidents of life.... After chatting a good deal, we suddenly all sank into silence. At such times they say an angel of peace is flying over.

I cannot say why my companions were silent, but I held my tongue because my eyes had suddenly come to rest on three dusty portraits in black wooden frames. The colours were rubbed and cracked in places, but one could still make out the faces. The portrait in the Centre was that of a young woman in a white gown with lace ruffles, her hair done up high, in the style of the eighties of last century. On her right, upon a perfectly black background, there stood out the full, round face of a good-natured country gentleman of five-and-twenty, with a broad, low brow, a thick nose, and a good-humoured smile. The French powdered coiffure was utterly out of keeping with the expression of his Slavonic face. The artist had portrayed him wearing a long loose coat of crimson colour with large paste buttons; in his hand he was holding some unlikely-looking flower. The third portrait, which was the work of some other more skillful hand, represented a man of thirty, in the green uniform, with red facings, of the time of Catherine, in a white shirt, with a fine cambric cravat. One hand leaned on a gold-headed cane, the other lay on his shirt front. His dark, thinnish face was full of insolent haughtiness. The fine long eyebrows almost grew together over the pitch-black eyes, about the thin, scarcely discernible lips played an evil smile.

'Why do you keep staring at those faces?' Piotr Fedoritch asked me.

'Oh, I don't know!' I answered, looking at him.

'Would you care to hear a whole story about those three persons?'

'Oh, please tell it,' we all responded with one voice.

Piotr Fedoritch got up, took a candle, carried it to the portraits, and in the tone of a showman at a wild beast show, 'Gentlemen!' he boomed, 'this lady was the adopted child of my great-grandfather, Olga Ivanovna N.N., called Lutchinov, who died forty years ago unmarried. This gentleman,' he pointed to the portrait of a man in uniform, 'served as a lieutenant in the Guards, Vassily Ivanovitch Lutchinov, expired by the will of God in the year seventeen hundred and ninety. And this gentleman, to whom I have not the honour of being related, is a certain Pavel Afanasiitch Rogatchov, serving nowhere, as far as I'm aware.... Kindly take note of the hole in his breast, just on the spot where the heart should be. That hole, you see, a regular three-sided hole, would be hardly likely to have come there by chance.... Now, 'he went on in his usual voice, 'kindly seat yourselves, arm yourselves with patience and listen.'

Gentlemen! (he began) I come of a rather old family. I am not proud of my descent, seeing that my ancestors were all fearful prodigals. Though that reproach cannot indeed be made against my great-grandfather, Ivan Andreevitch Lutchinov; on the contrary, he had the character of being excessively careful, even miserly—at any rate, in the latter years of his life. He spent his youth in Petersburg and lived through the reign of Elizabeth. In Petersburg he married, and had by his wife, my great-grandmother, four children, three sons, Vassily, Ivan, and Pavel, my grandfather, and one daughter, Natalia. In addition, Ivan Andreevitch took into his family the daughter of a distant relation, a nameless and destitute orphan—Olga Ivanovna, of whom I spoke just now. My great-grandfather's serfs were probably aware of his existence, for they used (when nothing particularly unlucky occurred) to send him a trifling rent, but they had never seen his face. The village of Lutchinovka, deprived of the bodily presence of its lord, was flourishing exceedingly, when all of a sudden one fine morning a cumbrous old family coach drove into the village and stopped before the elder's hut. The peasants, alarmed at such an unheard-of occurrence, ran up and saw their master and mistress and all their young ones, except the eldest, Vassily, who was left behind in Petersburg. From that memorable day down to the very day of his death, Ivan Andreevitch never left Lutchinovka. He built himself a house, the very house in which I have the pleasure of conversing with you at this moment. He built a church too and began living the life of a country gentleman. Ivan Andreevitch was a man of immense height, thin, silent, and very deliberate in all his movements. He never wore a dressing-gown, and no one but his valet had ever seen him without powder. Ivan Andreevitch usually walked with his hands clasped behind his back, turning his head at each step. Every day he used to walk in a long avenue of lime-trees, which he had planted with his own hand; and before his death he had the pleasure of enjoying the shade of those trees. Ivan Andreevitch was exceedingly sparing of his words; a proof of his taciturnity is to be found in the remarkable fact that in the course of twenty years he had not said a single word to his wife, Anna Pavlovna. His relations with Anna Pavlovna altogether were of a very curious sort. She directed the whole management of the household; at dinner she always sat beside her husband—he would mercilessly have chastised anyone who had dared to say a disrespectful word to her—and yet he never spoke to her, never touched her hand. Anna Pavlovna was a pale, broken-spirited woman, completely crushed. She prayed every day on her knees in church, and she never smiled. There was a rumour that they had formerly, that is, before they came into the country, lived on very cordial terms with one another. They did say too that Anna Pavlovna had been untrue to her matrimonial vows; that her conduct had come to her husband's knowledge.... Be that as it may, anyway Ivan Andreevitch, even when dying, was not reconciled to her. During his last illness, she never left him; but he seemed not to notice her. One night, Anna Pavlovna was sitting in Ivan Andreevitch's bedroom—he suffered from sleeplessness—a lamp was burning before the holy picture. My grandfather's servant, Yuditch, of whom I shall have to say a few words later, went out of the room. Anna Pavlovna got up, crossed the room, and sobbing flung herself on her knees at her husband's bedside, tried to say something—stretched out her hands... Ivan Andreevitch looked at her, and in a faint voice, but resolutely, called, 'Boy!' The servant went in; Anna Pavlovna hurriedly rose, and went back, tottering, to her place.

Ivan Andreevitch's children were exceedingly afraid of him. They grew up in the country, and were witnesses of Ivan Andreevitch's strange treatment of his wife. They all loved Anna Pavlovna passionately, but did not dare to show their love. She seemed of herself to hold aloof from them.... You remember my grandfather, gentlemen; to the day of his death, he always walked on tiptoe and spoke in a whisper... such is the force of habit! My grandfather and his brother, Ivan Ivanovitch, were simple, good-hearted people, quiet and depressed. My grand'tante Natalia married, as you are aware, a coarse, dull-witted man, and all her life she cherished an unutterable, slavish, sheep-like passion for him. But their brother Vassily was not of that sort. I believe I said that Ivan Andreevitch had left him in Petersburg. He was then twelve. His father confided him to the care of a distant kinsman, a man no longer young, a bachelor, and a terrible Voltairean.

Vassily grew up and went into the army. He was not tall but was well-built and exceedingly elegant; he spoke French excellently and was renowned for his skillful swordsmanship. He was considered one of the most brilliant young men of the beginning of the reign of Catherine. My father used often to tell me that he had known more than one old lady who could not refer to Vassily Ivanovitch Lutchinov without heartfelt emotion. Picture to yourselves a man endowed with exceptional strength of will, passionate and calculating, persevering and daring, reserved in the extreme, and—according to the testimony of all his contemporaries—fascinatingly, captivatingly attractive. He had no conscience, no heart, no principle, though no one could have called him positively a bad-hearted man. He was vain, but knew how to disguise his vanity, and passionately cherished his independence. When Vassily Ivanovitch would half close his black eyes, smiling affectionately, when he wanted to fascinate anyone, they say it was impossible to resist him; and even people, thoroughly convinced of the coldness and hardness of his heart, were more than once vanquished by the bewitching power of his personal influence. He served his own interests devotedly, and made other people, too, work for his advantage; and he was always successful in everything, because he never lost his head, never disdained using flattery as a means, and well understood how to use it.

Ten years after Ivan Andreevitch had settled in the country, he came for a four months' visit to Lutchinovka, a brilliant officer of the Guards, and in that time succeeded positively in turning the head of the grim old man, his father. Strange to say, Ivan Andreevitch listened with enjoyment to his son's stories of some of his *conquests*. His brothers were speechless in his presence and admired him as a being of a higher order. And Anna Pavlovna herself became almost fonder of him than any of her other children who were so sincerely devoted to her.

Vassily Ivanovitch had come down into the country primarily to visit his people, but also with the second object of getting as much money as possible from his father. He lived sumptuously in the glare of publicity in Petersburg and had made a mass of debts. He had no easy task to get round his father's miserliness, and though Ivan Andreevitch gave him on this one visit probably far more money than he gave all his other children together during twenty years spent under his roof, Vassily followed the well-known Russian rule, 'Get what you can!'

Ivan Andreevitch had a servant called Yuditch, just such another tall, thin, taciturn person as his master. They say that this man Yuditch was partly responsible for Ivan Andreevitch's strange behaviour with Anna Pavlovna; they say he discovered my great-grandmother's guilty intrigue with one of my great-grandfather's dearest friends. Most likely Yuditch deeply regretted his ill-timed jealousy, for it would be difficult to conceive a more kind-hearted man. His memory is held in veneration by all my house-serfs to this day. My great-grandfather put unbounded confidence in Yuditch. In those days landowners used to have money but did not put it into the keeping of banks, they kept it themselves in chests, under their floors, and so on. Ivan Andreevitch kept all his money in a great wrought-iron coffer, which stood under the head of his bed. The key of this coffer was intrusted to Yuditch. Every evening as he went to bed Ivan Andreevitch used to bid him open the coffer in his presence, used to tap in turn each of the tightly filled bags with a stick, and every Saturday he would untie the bags with Yuditch, and carefully count over the money. Vassily heard of all these doings and burned with eagerness to overhaul the sacred coffer. In the course of five or six days he had *softened* Yuditch, that is, he had worked on the old man till, as they say, he worshipped the ground his young master trod on. Having thus duly prepared him, Vassily put on a careworn and gloomy air, for a long while refused to answer Yuditch's questions and at last told him that he had lost at play and should make an end of himself if he could not get money somehow. Yuditch broke into sobs, flung himself on his knees before him, begged him to think of God, not to be his own ruin. Vassily locked himself in his room without uttering a word. A little while after he heard someone cautiously knocking at his door; he opened it, and saw in the doorway Yuditch pale and trembling, with the key in his hand. Vassily took in the whole position at a glance. At first, for a long while, he refused to take it. With tears Yuditch repeated, 'Take it, your honour, graciously take it!'... Vassily at last agreed. This took place on Monday. The idea occurred to Vassily to replace the money taken out with broken bits of crockery. He reckoned on Ivan Andreevitch's tapping the bags with his stick, and not noticing the hardly perceptible difference in the sound, and by Saturday he hoped to obtain and to replace the sum in the coffer. As he planned, so he did. His father did not, in fact, notice anything.

But by Saturday Vassily had not procured the money; he had hoped to win the sum from a rich neighbour at cards, and instead of that, he lost it all. Meantime, Saturday had come; it came at last to the turn of the bags filled with broken crocks. Picture, gentlemen, the amazement of Ivan Andreevitch!

'What does this mean?' he thundered. Yuditch was silent.

'You stole the money?'

'No, sir.'

'Then someone took the key from you?'

'I didn't give the key to anyone.'

'Not to anyone? Well then, you are the thief. Confess!'

'I am not a thief, Ivan Andreevitch.'

'Where did the devil these potsherds come from then? So, you're deceiving me! For the last time I tell you—confess!' Yuditch bowed his head and folded his hands behind his back.

'Hi, lads!' shrieked Ivan Andreevitch in a voice of frenzy. 'A stick!'

'What, beat... me?' murmured Yuditch.

'Yes, indeed! Are you any better than the rest? You are a thief! O Yuditch! I never expected such dishonesty of you!'

'I have grown grey in your service, Ivan Andreevitch,' Yuditch articulated with effort.

'What have I to do with your grey hairs? Damn you and your service!'

The servants came in.

'Take him, do, and give it him thoroughly.' Ivan Andreevitch's lips were white and twitching. He walked up and down the room like a wild beast in a small cage.

The servants did not dare to carry out his orders.

'Why are you standing still, children of Ham? Am I to undertake him myself, eh?'

Yuditch was moving towards the door....

'Stay!' screamed Ivan Andreevitch. 'Yuditch, for the last time I tell you, I beg you, Yuditch, confess!'

'I can't!' moaned Yuditch.

'Then take him, the sly old fox! Flog him to death! His blood be on my head!' thundered the infuriated old man. The flogging began.... The door suddenly opened, and Vassily came in. He was almost paler than his father, his hands were shaking, his upper lip was lifted, and laid bare a row of even, white teeth.

'I am to blame,' he said in a thick but resolute voice. 'I took the money.'

The servants stopped.

'You! what? you, Vaska! without Yuditch's consent?'

'No!' said Yuditch, 'with my consent. I gave Vassily Ivanovitch the key of my own accord. Your honour, Vassily Ivanovitch! why is your honour trouble?'

'So, this is the thief!' shrieked Ivan Andreevitch. 'Thanks, Vassily, thanks! But Yuditch, I'm not going to forgive you anyway. Why didn't you tell me all about it directly? Hey, you there! why are you standing still? do you too resist my authority? Ah, I'll settle things with you, my pretty gentleman!' he added, turning to Vassily.

The servants were again laying hands on Yuditch....

'Don't touch him!' murmured Vassily through his teeth. The men did not heed him. 'Back!' he shrieked and rushed upon them.... They stepped back.

'Ah! mutiny!' moaned Ivan Andreevitch, and, raising his stick, he approached his son. Vassily leaped back, snatched at the handle of his sword, and bared it to half its length. Everyone was trembling. Anna Pavlovna, attracted by the noise, showed herself at the door, pale and scared.

A terrible change passed over the face of Ivan Andreevitch. He tottered, dropped the stick, and sank heavily into an arm-chair, hiding his face in both hands. No one stirred, all stood rooted to the spot, Vassily like the rest. He clutched the steel sword-handle convulsively, and his eyes glittered with a weary, evil light....

'Go, all of you... all, out,' Ivan Andreevitch brought out in a low voice, not taking his hands from his face.

The whole crowd went out. Vassily stood still in the doorway, then suddenly tossed his head, embraced Yuditch, kissed his mother's hand... and two hours later he had left the place. He went back to Petersburg.

In the evening of the same day Yuditch was sitting on the steps of the house serfs' hut. The servants were all round him, sympathising with him and bitterly reproaching their young master.

'That's enough, lads,' he said to them at last, 'give over... why do you abuse him? He himself, the young master, I dare say is not very happy at his audacity....'

In consequence of this incident, Vassily never saw his father again. Ivan Andreevitch died without him, and died probably with such a load of sorrow on his heart as God grant none of us may ever know. Vassily Ivanovitch, meanwhile, went into the world, enjoyed himself in his own way, and squandered money recklessly. How he got hold of the money, I cannot tell for certain. He had obtained a French servant, a very smart and intelligent fellow, Bourcier, by name. This man was passionately attached to him and aided him in all his numerous manoeuvres. I do not intend to relate in detail all the exploits of my grand-uncle; he was possessed of such unbounded daring, such serpent-like resource, such inconceivable wiliness, such a fine and ready wit, that I must own I can understand the complete sway that the unprincipled person exercised even over the noblest natures.

Soon after his father's death, in spite of his wiliness, Vassily Ivanovitch was challenged by an injured husband. He fought a duel, seriously wounded his opponent, and was forced to leave the capital; he was banished to his estate and forbidden to leave it. Vassily Ivanovitch was thirty years old. You may easily imagine, gentlemen, with what feelings he left the brilliant life in the capital that he was used to and came into the country. They say that he got out of the hooded cart several times on the road, flung himself face downwards in the snow and cried. No one in Lutchinovka would have known him as the gay and charming Vassily Ivanovitch they had seen before. He did not talk to anyone; went out shooting from morning to night; endured his mother's timid caresses with undisguised impatience, and was merciless in his ridicule of his brothers, and of their wives (they were both married by that time)....

I have not so far, I think, told you anything about Olga Ivanovna. She had been brought as a tiny baby to Lutchinovka; she all but died on the road. Olga Ivanovna was brought up, as they say, in the fear of God and her betters. It must be admitted that Ivan Andreevitch and Anna Pavlovna both treated her as a daughter. But there lay hid in her soul a faint spark of that fire which burned so fiercely in Vassily Ivanovitch. While Ivan Andreevitch's own children did not dare even to wonder about the cause of the strange, dumb feud between their parents, Olga was from her earliest years disturbed and tormented by Anna Pavlovna's position. Like Vassily, she loved independence; any restriction fretted her. She was devoted with her whole soul to her benefactress; old Lutchinov she detested, and more than once, sitting at table, she shot such black looks at him, that even the servant handing the dishes felt uncomfortable. Ivan Andreevitch never noticed these glances, for he never took the slightest notice of his family.

At first Anna Pavlovna had tried to eradicate this hatred, but some bold questions of Olga's forced her to complete silence. The children of Ivan Andreevitch adored Olga, and the old lady too was fond of her, but not with a very ardent affection.

Long continued grieving had crushed all cheerfulness and every strong feeling in that poor woman; nothing is so clear a proof of Vassily's captivating charm as that he had made even his mother love him passionately. Demonstrations of tenderness on the part of children were not in the spirit of the age, and so it is not to be wondered at that Olga did not dare to express her devotion, though she always kissed Anna Pavlovna's hand with special reverence, when she said good-night to her. Twenty years later, Russian girls began to read romances of the class of *The Adventures of Marquis Glagol, Fanfan and Lolotta, Alexey or the Cottage in the Forest*; they began to play the clavichord and to sing songs in the style of the once very well-known:

'Men like butterflies in sunshine
Flutter round us opening blossoms,' etc.

But in the seventies of the last century (Olga Ivanovna was born in 1757) our country beauties had no notion of such accomplishments. It is difficult for us now to form a clear conception of the Russian miss of those days. We can indeed judge from our grandmothers of the degree of culture of girls of the noble family in the time of Catherine; but how is one to distinguish what they had gradually gained in the course of their long lives from what they were in the days of their youth?

Olga Ivanovna spoke French a little, but with a strong Russian accent: in her day there was as yet no talk of French emigrants. In fact, with all her fine qualities, she was still pretty much of a savage, and I dare say in the simplicity of her heart, she had more than once chastised some luckless servant girl with her own hands....

Sometime before Vassily Ivanovitch's arrival, Olga Ivanovna had been betrothed to a neighbour, Pavel Afanasievitch Rogatchov, a very good-natured and straightforward fellow. Nature had forgotten to put any spice of ill-temper into his composition. His own serfs did not obey him, and would sometimes all go off, down to the least of them, and leave poor Rogatchov without any dinner... but nothing could trouble the peace of his soul. From his childhood he had been stout and indolent, had never been in the government service, and was fond of going to church and singing in the choir. Look, gentlemen, at this round, good-natured face; glance at this mild, beaming smile... don't you really feel it reassuring, yourselves? His father used at long intervals to drive over to Lutchinovka, and on holidays used to bring with him his Pavlusha, whom the little Lutchinovs teased in every possible way. Pavlusha grew up, began driving over to call on Ivan Andreevitch on his own account, fell in love with Olga Ivanovna, and offered her his hand and heart—not to her personally, but to her benefactors. Her benefactors gave their consent. They never even thought of asking Olga Ivanovna whether she liked Rogatchov. In those days, in the words of my grandmother, 'such refinements were not the thing.' Olga soon got used to her betrothed, however; it was impossible not to feel fond of such a gentle and amiable creature. Rogatchov had received no education whatever; his French consisted of the one word *bonjour*, and he secretly considered even that word improper. But some jocose person had taught him the following lines, as a French song: 'Sonitchka, Sonitchka! Ke-voole-voo-de-mwa—I adore you—me-je-ne-pyoo-pa....' This supposed song he always used to hum to himself when he felt in good spirits. His father was also a man of incredibly good-nature, always wore a long Nankin coat and whatever was said to him he responded with a smile. From the time of Pavel Afanasievitch's betrothal, both the Rogatchovs, father and son, had been tremendously busy. They had been having their house entirely transformed adding various 'galleries,' talking in a friendly way with the workmen, encouraging them with drinks. They had not yet completed all these additions by the winter; they put off the wedding till the summer. In the summer Ivan Andreevitch died; the wedding was deferred till the following spring. In the winter Vassily Ivanovitch arrived. Rogatchov was presented to him; he received him coldly and contemptuously, and as time went on, he, so alarmed him by his haughty behaviour that poor Rogatchov trembled like a leaf at the very sight of him, was tongue-tied and smiled nervously. Vassily once almost annihilated him altogether—by making him a bet, that he, Rogatchov, was not able to stop smiling. Poor Pavel Afanasievitch almost cried with embarrassment, but—actually!—a smile, a stupid, nervous smile refused to leave his perspiring face! Vassily toyed deliberately with the ends of his neckerchief and looked at him with supreme contempt. Pavel Afanasievitch's father heard too of Vassily's presence, and after an interval of a few days—'for the sake of greater formality'—he sallied off to Lutchinovka with the object of 'felicitating our honoured guest on his advent to the halls of his ancestors.' Afanasey Lukitch was famed all over the countryside for his eloquence that is to say, for his capacity for enunciating without faltering a rather long and complicated speech, with a sprinkling of bookish phrases in it. Alas! on this occasion he did not sustain his reputation; he was even more disconcerted than his son, Pavel Afanasievitch; he mumbled something quite inarticulate, and though he had never been used to taking vodka, he at once drained a glass 'to carry things off'—he found Vassily at lunch,—tried at least to clear his throat with some dignity, and did not succeed in making the slightest sound. On their way home, Pavel Afanasievitch whispered to his parent, 'Well, father?' Afanasey Lukitch responded angrily also in a whisper, 'Don't speak of it!'

The Rogatchovs began to be less frequent visitors at Lutchinovka. Though indeed they were not the only people intimidated by Vassily; he awakened in his own brothers, in their wives, in Anna Pavlovna herself, an instinctive feeling of uneasiness and discomfort... they tried to avoid him in every way they could. Vassily must have noticed this, but apparently had no intention of altering his behaviour to them. Suddenly, at the beginning of the spring, he became once more the charming, attractive person they had known of old...

The first symptom of this sudden transformation was Vassily's unexpected visit to the Rogatchovs. Afanasey Lukitch, in particular, was fairly disconcerted at the sight of Lutchinov's carriage, but his dismay very quickly vanished. Never had Vassily been more courteous and delightful. He took young Rogatchov by the arm, went with him to look at the new buildings, talked to the carpenters, made some suggestions, with his own hands chopped a few chips off with the axe, asked to be shown Afanasey Lukitch's stud horses, himself trotted them out on a halter, and altogether so affected the good-hearted children of the steppes by his gracious affability that they both embraced him more than once. At home, too, Vassily managed, in the course of a few days, to turn every one's head just as before. He contrived all sorts of laughable games, got hold of musicians, invited the ladies and gentlemen of the neighbourhood, told the old ladies the scandals of the town in the most amusing way, flirted a little with the young ones, invented unheard-of diversions, fireworks and such things, in short, he put life into everything and everyone. The melancholy, gloomy house of the Lutchinovs was suddenly converted into a noisy, brilliant, enchanted palace of which the whole countryside was talking. This sudden transformation surprised many and delighted all. All sorts of rumours began to be whispered about. Sagacious persons opined that Vassily Ivanovitch had till then been crushed under the weight of some secret trouble, that he saw chances of returning to the capital... but the true cause of Vassily Ivanovitch's metamorphosis was guessed by no one.

Olga Ivanovna, gentlemen, was rather pretty; though her beauty consisted rather in the extraordinary softness and freshness of her shape, in the quiet grace of her movements than in the strict regularity of her features. Nature had bestowed on her a certain independence; her bringing up—she had grown up without a father or mother—had developed in her reserve and determination. Olga did not belong to the class of quiet and tame-spirited young ladies; but only one feeling had reached its full possibilities in her as yet—hatred for her benefactor. Other more feminine passions might indeed flare up in Olga Ivanovna's heart with abnormal and painful violence... but she had not the cold pride, nor the intense strength of will, nor the self-centred egoism, without which any passion passes quickly away.

The first rush of feeling in such half-active, half-passive natures is sometimes extremely violent; but they give way very quickly, especially when it is a question of relentless conformity with accepted principles; they are afraid of consequences.... And yet, gentlemen, I will frankly confess, women of that sort always make the strongest impression on me. ... (At these words the speaker drank a glass of water. Rubbish! rubbish! I thought, looking at his round chin; nothing in the world makes a strong impression on you, my dear fellow!)

Piotr Fedoritch resumed: Gentlemen, I believe in blood, in race. Olga Ivanovna had more blood than, for instance, her foster sister, Natalia. How did this blood show itself; do you ask? Why, in everything; in the lines of her hands, in her lips, in the sound of her voice, in her glance, in her carriage, in her hair, in the very folds of her gown. In all these trifles there lay hid something special, though I am bound to admit that the—how can one express it?—*la distinction*, which had fallen to Olga Pavlovna's share would not have attracted Vassily's notice had he met her in Petersburg. But in the country, in the wilds, she not only caught his attention, but she was also positively the sole cause of the transformation of which I have just been speaking.

Consider the position. Vassily Ivanovitch liked to enjoy life; he could not but be bored in the country; his brothers were good-natured fellows, but extremely limited people: he had nothing in common with them. His sister, Natalia, with the assistance of her husband, had brought into the world in the course of three years no less than four babies; between her and Vassily was a perfect gulf.... Anna Pavlovna went to church, prayed, fasted, and was preparing herself for death. There remained only Olga—a fresh, shy, pretty girl.... Vassily did not notice her at first... indeed, who does notice a dependant, an orphan girl kept from charity in the house?... One day, at the very beginning of spring, Vassily was walking about the garden, and with his cane slashing off the heads of the dandelions, those stupid yellow flowers, which come out first in such numbers in the meadows, as soon as they begin to grow green. He was walking in the garden in front of the house; he lifted his head and caught sight of Olga Ivanovna.

She was sitting sideways at the window, dreamily stroking a tabby kitten, who, purring and blinking, nestled on her lap, and with great satisfaction held up her little nose into the rather hot spring sunshine. Olga Ivanovna was wearing a white morning gown, with short sleeves; her bare, pale-pink, girlish shoulders and arms were a picture of freshness and health. A little red cap discreetly restrained her thick, soft, silky curls. Her face was a little flushed; she was only just awake. Her slender, flexible neck bent forward so charmingly; there was such seductive negligence, such modesty in the restful pose of her figure, free from corsets, that Vassily Ivanovitch (a great connoisseur!) halted involuntarily and peeped in. It suddenly occurred to him that Olga Ivanovna ought not to be left in her primitive ignorance; that she might with time be turned into a very sweet and charming woman. He stole up to the window, stretched up on tiptoe and imprinted a silent kiss on Olga Ivanovna's smooth, white arm, a little below the elbow.

Olga shrieked and jumped up, the kitten put its tail in the air and leaped into the garden. Vassily Ivanovitch with a smile kept her by the arm.... Olga flushed all over, to her ears; he began to rally her on her alarm... invited her to come a walk with him. But Olga Ivanovna became suddenly conscious of the negligence of her attire, and 'swifter than the swift red deer' she slipped away into the next room.

The very same day Vassily set off to the Rogatchovs. He was suddenly happy and light-hearted. Vassily was not in love with Olga, no! the word 'love' is not to be used lightly.... He had found an occupation, had set himself a task, and rejoiced with the delight of a man of action. He did not even remember that she was his mother's ward, and another man's betrothed. He never for one instant deceived himself; he was fully aware that it was not for her to be his wife.... Possibly there was passion to excuse him—not a very elevated nor noble passion, truly, but still a fairly strong and tormenting passion. Of course he was not in love like a boy; he did not give way to vague ecstasies; he knew very well what he wanted and what he was striving for.

Vassily was a perfect master of the art of winning over, in the shortest time, any one however shy or prejudiced against him. Olga soon ceased to be shy with him. Vassily Ivanovitch led her into a new world. He ordered a clavichord for her, gave her music lessons (he himself played fairly well on the flute), read books aloud to her, had long conversations with her.... The poor child of the steppes soon had her head turned completely. Vassily dominated her entirely. He knew how to tell her of what had been till then unknown to her and to tell her in a language she could understand. Olga little by little gained courage to express all her feelings to him: he came to her aid, helped her out with the words she could not find, did not alarm her, at one moment kept her back, at another encouraged her confidences.... Vassily busied himself with her education from no disinterested desire to awaken and develop her talents. He simply wanted to draw her a little closer to himself; and he knew too that an innocent, shy, but vain young girl is more easily seduced through the mind than the heart. Even if Olga had been an exceptional being, Vassily would never have perceived it, for he treated her like a child. But as you are aware, gentlemen, there was nothing specially remarkable in Olga. Vassily tried all he could to work on her imagination, and often in the evening she left his side with such a whirl of new images, phrases and ideas in her head that she could not sleep all night, but lay breathing uneasily and turning her burning cheeks from side to side on the cool pillows, or got up, went to the window and gazed fearfully and eagerly into the dark distance. Vassily filled every moment of her life; she could not think of anyone else. As for Rogatchov, she soon positively ceased to notice his existence. Vassily had the tact and shrewdness not to talk to Olga in his presence; but he either made him laugh till he was ready to cry, or arranged some noisy entertainment, a riding expedition, a boating party by night with torches and music—he did not in fact let Pavel Afanasievitch have a chance to think clearly.

But in spite of all Vassily Ivanovitch's tact, Rogatchov dimly felt that he, Olga's betrothed and future husband, had somehow become as if it were an outsider to her... but in the boundless goodness of his heart, he was afraid of wounding her by reproaches, though he sincerely loved her and prized her affection. When left alone with her, he did not know what to say, and only tried all he could to follow her wishes. Two months passed by. Every trace of self-reliance, of will, disappeared at last in Olga. Rogatchov, feeble and tongue-tied, could be no support to her. She had no wish even to resist the enchantment, and with a sinking heart she surrendered unconditionally to Vassily....

Olga Ivanovna may very likely then have known something of the bliss of love; but it was not for long. Though Vassily—for lack of other occupation—did not drop her, and even attached himself to her and looked after her fondly, Olga herself was so utterly distraught that she found no happiness even in love and yet could not tear herself away from Vassily. She began to be frightened at everything, did not dare to think, could talk of nothing, gave up reading, and was devoured by misery. Sometimes Vassily succeeded in carrying her along with him and making her forget everything and everyone. But the very next day he would find her pale, speechless, with icy hands, and a fixed smile on her lips.... There followed a time of some difficulty for Vassily; but no difficulties could dismay him. He concentrated himself like a skilled gambler. He could not in the least rely upon Olga Ivanovna; she was continually betraying herself, turning pale, blushing, weeping... her new part was utterly beyond her powers. Vassily toiled for two: in his restless and boisterous gaiety, only an experienced observer could have detected something strained and feverish. He played his brothers, sisters, the Rogatchovs, the neighbours, like pawns at chess. He was everlastingly on the alert. Not a single glance, a single movement, was lost on him, yet he appeared the most heedless of men. Every morning, he faced the fray and every evening he scored a victory. He was not the least oppressed by such a fearful strain of activity. He slept four hours out of the twenty-four, ate very little, and was healthy, fresh, and good-humoured.

Meantime the wedding-day was approaching. Vassily succeeded in persuading Pavel Afanasievitch himself of the necessity of delay. Then he dispatched him to Moscow to make various purchases, while he was himself in correspondence with friends in Petersburg. He took all this trouble, not so much from sympathy for Olga Ivanovna, as from a natural bent and liking for bustle and agitation.... Besides, he was beginning to be sick of Olga Ivanovna, and more than once after a violent outbreak of passion for her, he would look at her, as he sometimes did at Rogatchov. Lutchinov always remained a riddle to everyone. In the coldness of his relentless soul, you felt the presence of a strange almost southern fire, and even in the wildest glow of passion a breath of icy chill seemed to come from the man.

Before other people he supported Olga Ivanovna as before. But when they were alone, he played with her like a cat with a mouse, or frightened her with sophistries, or was wearily, malignantly bored, or again flung himself at her feet, swept her away, like a straw in a hurricane... and there was no feigning at such moments in his passion... he really was moved himself.

One day, rather late in the evening, Vassily was sitting alone in his room, attentively reading over the last letters he had received from Petersburg, when suddenly he heard a faint creak at the door, and Olga Ivanovna's maid, Palashka, came in.

'What do you want?' Vassily asked her rather crossly.

'My mistress begs you to come to her.'

'I can't just now. Go along.... Well, what are you standing there for?' he went on, seeing that Palashka did not go away.

'My mistress told me to say that she very particularly wants to see you,' she said.

'Why, what's the matter?'

'Would your honour please to see for yourself....'

Vassily got up, angrily flung the letters into a drawer, and went into Olga Ivanovna. She was sitting alone in a corner, pale and passive.

'What do you want?' he asked her, not quite politely.

Olga looked at him and closed her eyes.

'What's the matter? what is it, Olga?'

He took her hand.... Olga Ivanovna's hand was cold as ice... She tried to speak... and her voice died away. The poor woman had no possible doubt of her condition left her.

Vassily was a little disconcerted. Olga Ivanovna's room was a couple of steps from Anna Pavlovna's bedroom. Vassily cautiously sat down by Olga, kissed and chafed her hands, comforted her in whispers. She listened to him, and silently, faintly, shuddered. In the doorway stood Palashka, stealthily wiping her eyes. In the next room they heard the heavy, even ticking of the clock, and the breathing of someone asleep. Olga Ivanovna's numbness dissolved at last into tears and stifled sobs. Tears are like a storm; after them one is always calmer. When Olga Ivanovna had quieted down a little, and only sobbed convulsively at intervals, like a child, Vassily knelt before her with caresses and tender promises, soothed her completely, gave her something to drink, put her to bed, and went away. He did not undress all night; wrote two or three letters, burnt two or three papers, took out a gold locket containing the portrait of a black-browed, black-eyed woman with a bold, voluptuous face, scrutinised her features slowly, and walked up and down the room pondering.

Next day, at breakfast, he saw with extreme displeasure poor Olga's red and swollen eyes and pale, agitated face. After breakfast he proposed a stroll in the garden to her. Olga followed Vassily, like a submissive sheep. When two hours afterwards she came in from the garden she quite broke down; she told Anna Pavlovna she was unwell and went to lie down on her bed. During their walk Vassily had, with a suitable show of remorse, informed her that he was secretly married—he was really as much a bachelor as I am. Olga Ivanovna did not fall into a swoon—people don't fall into swoons except on the stage—but she turned all at once stony, though she herself was so far from hoping to marry Vassily Ivanovitch that she was even afraid to think about it. Vassily had begun to explain to her the inevitableness of her parting from him and marrying Rogatchov. Olga Ivanovna looked at him in dumb horror. Vassily talked in a cool, business-like, practical way, blamed himself, expressed his regret, but concluded all his remarks with the following words: 'There's no going back on the past; we've got to act.'

Olga was utterly overwhelmed; she was filled with terror and shame; a dull, heavy despair came upon her; she longed for death and waited in agony for Vassily's decision.

'We must confess everything to my mother,' he said to her at last.

Olga turned deadly pale; her knees shook under her.

'Don't be afraid, don't be afraid,' repeated Vassily, 'trust to me, I won't desert you... I will make everything right... rely upon me.'

The poor woman looked at him with love... yes, with love, and deep, but hopeless devotion.

'I will arrange everything, everything,' Vassily said to her at parting... and for the last time he kissed her chilly hands....

Next morning—Olga Ivanovna had only just risen from her bed—her door opened... and Anna Pavlovna appeared in the doorway. She was supported by Vassily. In silence she got as far as an arm-chair, and in silence she sat down. Vassily stood at her side. He looked composed; his brows were knitted, and his lips slightly parted. Anna Pavlovna, pale, indignant, angry, tried to speak, but her voice failed her. Olga Ivanovna glanced in horror from her benefactress to her lover, with a terrible sinking at her heart... she fell on her knees with a shriek in the middle of the room and hid her face in her hands.

'Then it's true... is it true?' murmured Anna Pavlovna and bent down to her.... 'Answer!' she went on harshly, clutching Olga by the arm.

'Mother!' rang out Vassily's brazen voice, 'you promised me not to be hard on her.'

'I want... confess... confess... is it true? Is it true?'

'Mother... remember...' Vassily began deliberately.

This one word moved Anna Pavlovna greatly. She leaned back in her chair and burst into sobs.

Olga Ivanovna softly raised her head and would have flung herself at the old lady's feet, but Vassily kept her back, raised her from the ground, and led her to another arm-chair. Anna Pavlovna went on weeping and muttering disconnected words....

'Come, mother,' began Vassily, 'don't torment yourself, the trouble may yet be set right.... If Rogatchov...'

Olga Ivanovna shuddered and drew herself up.

'If Rogatchov,' pursued Vassily, with a meaning glance at Olga Ivanovna, 'imagines that he can disgrace an honourable family with impunity...'

Olga Ivanovna was overcome with horror.

'In my house,' moaned Anna Pavlovna.

'Calm yourself, mother. He took advantage of her innocence, her youth, he—you wish to say something'—he broke off, seeing that Olga made a movement towards him....

Olga Ivanovna sank back in her chair.

'I will go to Rogatchov once. I will make him marry her this very day. You may be sure I will not let him make a laughing-stock of us....'

'But... Vassily Ivanovitch... you...' whispered Olga.

He gave her a prolonged, cold stare. She sank into silence again.

'Mother, give me your word not to worry her before I return. Look, she is half dead. And you, too, must rest. Rely upon me; I answer for everything; in any case, wait till I return. I tell you again, don't torture her, or yourself, and trust to me.'

He went to the door and stopped. 'Mother,' he said, 'come with me, leave her alone, I beg of you.'

Anna Pavlovna got up, went up to the holy picture, bowed down to the ground, and slowly followed her son. Olga Ivanovna, without a word or a movement, looked after them.

Vassily turned back quickly, snatched her hand, whispered in her ear, 'Rely on me, and don't betray us,' and at once withdrew.... 'Bourcier!' he called, running swiftly down the stairs, 'Bourcier!'

A quarter of an hour later he was sitting in his carriage with his valet.

That day the elder Rogatchov was not at home. He had gone to the district town to buy cloth for the liveries of his servants. Pavel Afanasievitch was sitting in his own room, looking through a collection of faded butterflies. With lifted eyebrows and protruding lips, he was carefully, with a pin, turning over the fragile wings of a 'night sphinx' moth, when he was suddenly aware of a small but heavy hand on his shoulder. He looked round. Vassily stood before him.

'Good-morning, Vassily Ivanovitch,' he said in some amazement.

Vassily looked at him and sat down on a chair facing him.

Pavel Afanasievitch was about to smile... but he glanced at Vassily and subsided with his mouth open, and his hands clasped.

'Tell me, Pavel Afanasievitch,' said Vassily suddenly, 'are you meaning to dance at your *wedding soon?*'

'I?... soon... of course... for my part... though as you and your sister ... I, for my part, am ready tomorrow even.'

'Very good, very good. You're a very impatient person, Pavel Afanasievitch.'

'How so?'

'Let me tell you,' pursued Vassily Ivanovitch, getting up, 'I know all; you understand me, and I order you without delay tomorrow to marry Olga.'

'Excuse me, excuse me,' objected Rogatchov, not rising from his seat; 'you order me. I sought Olga Ivanovna's hand of myself and there's no need to give me orders.... I confess, Vassily Ivanovitch, I don't quite understand you.'

'You don't understand me?'

'No, really, I don't understand you.'

'Do you give me your word to marry her tomorrow?'

'Why, mercy on us, Vassily Ivanovitch... haven't you yourself put off our wedding more than once? Except for you it would have taken place long ago. And now I have no idea of breaking it off. What is the meaning of your threats, your insistence?'

Pavel Afanasievitch wiped the sweat off his face.

'Do you give me your word? Say yes or no!' Vassily repeated emphatically.

'Excuse me... I will... but...'

'Very good. Remember then... She has confessed everything.'

'Who has confessed?'

'Olga Ivanovna.'

'Why, what has she confessed?'

'Why, what are you pretending to me for, Pavel Afanasievitch? I'm not a stranger to you.'

'What am I pretending? I don't understand you, I don't, I positively don't understand a word. What could Olga Ivanovna confess?'

'What? You are really too much! You know what.'

'May God slay me...'

'No, I'll slay you, if you don't marry her... do you understand?'

'What!...' Pavel Afanasievitch jumped up and stood facing Vassily. 'Olga Ivanovna... you tell me...'

'You're a clever fellow, you are, I must own'—Vassily with a smile patted him on the shoulder—'though you do look so innocent.'

'Good God!... You'll send me out of my mind.... What do you mean, explain, for God's sake!'

Vassily bent down and whispered something in his ear.

Rogatchov cried out, 'What!...!?'

Vassily stamped.

'Olga Ivanovna? Olga?...'

'Yes... your betrothed...'

'My betrothed... Vassily Ivanovitch... she... she... Why, I never wish to see her again,' cried Pavel Afanasievitch. 'Good-bye to her forever! What do you take me for? I'm being duped... I'm being duped... Olga Ivanovna, how wrong of you, have you no shame?...' (Tears gushed from his eyes.) 'Thanks, Vassily Ivanovitch, thanks very much... I never wish to see her again now! no! no! don't speak of her.... Ah, merciful Heavens! to think I have lived to see this! Oh, very well, very well!'

'That's enough nonsense,' Vassily Ivanovitch observed coldly. 'Remember, you've given me your word: the wedding's tomorrow.'

'No, that it won't be! Enough of that, Vassily Ivanovitch. I say again, what do you take me for? You do me too much honour. I'm humbly obliged. Excuse me.'

'As you please!' retorted Vassily. 'Get your sword.'

'Sword... what for?'

'What for?... I'll show you what for.'

Vassily drew out his fine, flexible French sword and bent it a little against the floor.

'You want... to fight... me?'

'Precisely so.'

'But Vassily Ivanovitch, put yourself in my place! How can I, only think, after what you have just told me.... I'm a man of honour, Vassily Ivanovitch, a nobleman.'

'You're a nobleman, you're a man of honour, so you'll be so good as to fight with me.'

'Vassily Ivanovitch!'

'You are frightened, I think, Mr. Rogatchov.'

'I'm not in the least frightened, Vassily Ivanovitch. You thought you would frighten me, Vassily Ivanovitch. I'll scare him, you thought, he's a coward, and he'll agree to anything directly... No, Vassily Ivanovitch, I am a nobleman as much as you are, though I've not had city breeding, and you won't succeed in frightening me into anything, excuse me.'

'Very good,' retorted Vassily; 'where is your sword then?'

'Eroshka!' shouted Pavel Afanasievitch. A servant came in.

'Get me the sword—there—you know, in the loft... make haste....'

Eroshka went out. Pavel Afanasievitch suddenly became exceedingly pale, hurriedly took off his dressing-gown, put on a reddish coat with big paste buttons... twisted a cravat round his neck... Vassily looked at him, and twiddled the fingers of his right hand.

'Well, are we to fight then, Pavel Afanasievitch?'

'Let's fight, if we must fight,' replied Rogatchov, and hurriedly buttoned up his shirt.

'Ay, Pavel Afanasievitch, you take my advice, marry her... what is it to you... And believe me, I'll...'

'No, Vassily Ivanovitch,' Rogatchov interrupted him. 'You'll kill me or maim me, I know, but I'm not going to lose my honour; if I'm to die then I must die.'

Eroshka came in, and trembling, gave Rogatchov a wretched old sword in a torn leather scabbard. In those days all noblemen wore swords with powder, but in the steppes they only put on powder twice a year. Eroshka moved away to the door and burst out crying. Pavel Afanasievitch pushed him out of the room.

'But Vassily Ivanovitch,' he observed with some embarrassment, 'I can't fight with you on the spot: allow me to put off our duel till tomorrow. My father is not at home, and it would be as well for me to put my affairs in order to—to be ready for anything.'

'I see you're beginning to feel frightened again, sir.'

'No, no, Vassily Ivanovitch; but consider yourself...'

'Listen!' shouted Lutchinov, 'you drive me out of patience.... Either give me your word to marry her at once, or fight...or I'll thrash you with my cane like a coward,—do you understand?'

'Come into the garden,' Rogatchov answered through his teeth.

But all at once the door opened, and the old nurse, Efimovna, utterly distracted, broke into the room, fell on her knees before Rogatchov, and clasped his legs....

'My little master!' she wailed, 'my nursling... what is it you are about? Will you be the death of us poor wretches, your honour? Sure, he'll kill you, darling! Only you say the word, you say the word, and we'll make an end of him, the insolent fellow.... Pavel Afanasievitch, my baby-boy, for the love of God!'

A number of pale, excited faces showed in the door...there was even the red beard of the village elder...

'Let me go, Efimovna, let me go!' muttered Rogatchov.

'I won't, my own, I won't. What are you about, sir, what are you about? What'll Afanasey Lukitch say? Why, he'll drive us all out of the light of day.... Why are you fellows standing still? Take the uninvited guest in hand and show him out of the house, so that not a trace be left of him.'

'Rogatchov!' Vassily Ivanovitch shouted menacingly.

'You are crazy, Efimovna, you are shaming me, come, come...' said Pavel Afanasievitch. 'Go away, go away, in God's name and you others, off with you, do you hear?...'

Vassily Ivanovitch moved swiftly to the open window, took out a small silver whistle, blew lightly... Bourcier answered from close by. Lutchinov turned at once to Pavel Afanasievitch.

'What's to be the end of this farce?'

'Vassily Ivanovitch, I will come to you tomorrow. What can I do with this crazy old woman?...'

'Oh, I see it's no good wasting words on you,' said Vassily, and he swiftly raised his cane...

Pavel Afanasievitch broke loose, pushed Efimovna away, snatched up the sword, and rushed through another door into the garden.

Vassily dashed after him. They ran into a wooden summerhouse, painted cunningly after the Chinese fashion, shut themselves in, and drew their swords. Rogatchov had once taken lessons in fencing, but now he was scarcely capable of drawing a sword properly. The blades crossed. Vassily was obviously playing with Rogatchov's sword. Pavel Afanasievitch was breathless and pale and gazed in consternation into Lutchinov's face.

Meanwhile, screams were heard in the garden; a crowd of people were running to the summerhouse. Suddenly Rogatchov heard the heart-rending wail of old age...he recognised the voice of his father. Afanasey Lukitch, bare-headed, with dishevelled hair, was running in front of them all, frantically waving his hands....

With a violent and unexpected turn of the blade Vassily sent the sword flying out of Pavel Afanasievitch's hand.

'Marry her, my boy,' he said to him: 'give over this foolery!'

'I won't marry her,' whispered Rogatchov, and he shut his eyes, and shook all over.

Afanasey Lukitch began banging at the door of the summerhouse.

'You won't?' shouted Vassily.

Rogatchov shook his head.

'Well, damn you, then!'

Poor Pavel Afanasievitch fell dead: Lutchinov's sword stabbed him to the heart... The door gave way; old Rogatchov burst into the summerhouse, but Vassily had already jumped out of window...

Two hours later he went into Olga Ivanovna's room... She rushed in terror to meet him... He bowed to her in silence; took out his sword and pierced Pavel Afanasievitch's portrait in the place of the heart. Olga shrieked and fell unconscious on the floor... Vassily went into Anna Pavlovna. He found her in the oratory. 'Mother,' said he, 'we are avenged.' The poor old woman shuddered and went on praying.

Within a week Vassily had returned to Petersburg, and two years later he came back stricken with paralysis—tongue-tied. He found neither Anna Pavlovna nor Olga living, and soon after died himself in the arms of Yuditch, who fed him like a child, and was the only one who could understand his incoherent stuttering.

1846.

THE DOG

"But if we can admit the possibility of the supernatural, the possibility of its intervention in real life,—then allow me to inquire, what role is sound judgment bound to play after this?"—shouted Antón Stepánitch, crossing his arms on his stomach.

Antón Stepánitch had held the rank of State Councillor,[1] had served in some wonderful department, and, as his speech was interlarded with pauses and was slow and uttered in a bass voice, he enjoyed universal respect. Not long before the date of our story, "the good-for-nothing little Order of St. Stanislas had been stuck on him," as those who envied him expressed it.

"That is perfectly just,"—remarked Skvorévitch.

"No one will dispute that,"—added Kinarévitch.

"I assent also,"—chimed in, in falsetto, from a corner the master of the house, Mr. Finopléntoff.

"But I, I must confess, cannot assent, because something supernatural has happened to me,"—said a man of medium stature and middle age, with a protruding abdomen and a bald spot, who had been sitting silent before the stove up to that moment. The glances of all present in the room were turned upon him with curiosity and surprise—and silence reigned.

This man was a landed proprietor of Kalúga, not wealthy, who had recently come to Petersburg. He had once served in the hussars, had gambled away his property, resigned from the service and settled down in the country. The recent agricultural changes had cut off his revenues, and he had betaken himself to the capital in search of a snug little position. He possessed no abilities and had no influential connections; but he placed great reliance on the friendship of an old comrade in the service, who had suddenly, without rhyme or reason, become a person of importance, and whom he had once aided to administer a sound thrashing to a card-sharper. Over and above that he counted upon his own luck—and it had not betrayed him; several days later he obtained the post of inspector of government storehouses, a profitable, even honourable position which did not require extraordinary talents: the storehouses themselves existed only in contemplation, and no one even knew with certainty what they were to contain,—but they had been devised as a measure of governmental economy.

Antón Stepánitch was the first to break the general silence.

"What, my dear sir?"—he began. "Do you seriously assert that something supernatural—I mean to say, incompatible with the laws of nature—has happened to you?"

"I do,"—returned "my dear sir," whose real name was Porfíry Kapítonitch.

"Incompatible with the laws of nature?"—energetically repeated Antón Stepánitch, who evidently liked that phrase.

"Precisely … yes; precisely the sort of thing you allude to."

"This is astonishing! What think you, gentlemen?"—Antón Stepánitch endeavoured to impart to his features an ironical expression, but without result—or, to speak more accurately, the only result was to produce the effect that Mr. State Councillor smelt a bad odour.—"Will not you be so kind, my dear sir,"—he went on, addressing the landed proprietor from Kalúga,—"as to communicate to us the particulars of such a curious event?"

"Why not? Certainly!"—replied the landed proprietor, and moving forward to the middle of the room in an easy manner he spoke as follows:

I have, gentlemen, as you are probably aware,—or as you may not be aware,—a small estate in Kozyól County. I formerly derived some profit from it—but now, of course, nothing but unpleasantness is to be anticipated. However, let us put politics aside! Well, sir, on that same estate I have a "wee little" manor: a vegetable garden, as is proper, a tiny pond with little carp, and some sort of buildings—well, and a small wing for my own sinful body.... I am a bachelor. So, sir, one day—about six years ago—I had returned home rather late; I had been playing cards at a neighbour's house—but I beg you to observe, I was not tipsy, as the expression goes. I undressed, got into bed, and blew out the light. And just imagine, gentlemen; no sooner had I blown out the light, than something began to rummage under my bed! Is it a rat? I thought. No, it was not a rat: it clawed and fidgeted and scratched itself.... At last, it began to flap its ears!

It was a dog—that was clear. But where had the dog come from? I keep none myself. "Can some stray animal have run in?" I thought. I called to my servant; his name is Fílka. The man entered with a candle.

"What's this,"—says I,—"my good Fílka? How lax thou art! A dog has intruded himself under my bed."

"What dog?"—says he.

"How should I know?"—says I;—"that's thy affair—not to allow thy master to be disturbed."

My Fílka bent down and began to pass the candle about under the bed.

"Why,"—says he,—"there's no dog here."

I bent down also; in fact, there was no dog.... Here was a marvel! I turned my eyes on Fílka: he was smiling.

"Fool,"—said I to him,—"what art thou grinning about? When thou didst open the door the dog probably took and sneaked out into the anteroom. But thou, gaper, didst notice nothing, because thou art eternally asleep. Can it be that thou thinkest I am drunk?"

He attempted to reply, but I drove him out, curled myself up in a ring, and heard nothing more that night.

But on the following night—just imagine!—the same thing was repeated. No sooner had I blown out the light than it began to claw and flap its ears. Again, I summoned Fílka, again he looked under the bed—again nothing! I sent him away, blew out the light—phew, damn it! there was the dog still. And a dog it certainly was I could hear it breathing and rummaging in its hair with its teeth in search of fleas so plainly!

"Fílka!"—says I,—"come hither without a light!"… He entered…. "Well, now,"—says I, "dost thou hear?…"

"I do,"—said he. I could not see him, but I felt that the fellow was quailing.

"What dost thou make of it?"—said I.

"What dost thou command me to make of it, Porfíry Kapítonitch?… 'Tis an instigation of the Evil One!"

"Thou art a lewd fellow; hold thy tongue with thy instigation of the Evil One."… But the voices of both of us were like those of birds, and we were shaking as though in a fever—in the darkness. I lighted a candle: there was no dog, and no noise whatever—only Fílka and I as white as clay. And I must inform you, gentlemen—you can believe me or not—but from that night forth for the space of six weeks the same thing went on. At last, I even got accustomed to it and took to extinguishing my light because I cannot sleep with a light. "Let him fidget!" I thought. "It doesn't harm me."

"But—I see—that you do not belong to the cowardly squad,"—interrupted Antón Stepánitch, with a half-scornful, half-condescending laugh. "The hussar is immediately perceptible!"

"I should not be frightened at you, in any case,"—said Porfíry Kapítonitch, and for a moment he really did look like a hussar.—"But listen further."

A neighbour came to me, the same one with whom I was in the habit of playing cards. He dined with me on what God had sent and lost fifty rubles to me for his visit; night was drawing on—it was time for him to go. But I had calculations of my own:—"Stop and spend the night with me, Vasíly Vasílitch; tomorrow thou wilt win it back, God willing."

My Vasíly Vasílitch pondered and pondered—and stayed. I ordered a bed to be placed for him in my own chamber…. Well, sir, we went to bed, smoked, chattered,—chiefly about the feminine sex, as is fitting in bachelor society,—and laughed, as a matter of course. I look; Vasíly Vasílitch has put out his candle and has turned his back on me; that signifies: "*Schlafen Sie wohl.*" I waited a little and extinguished my candle also. And imagine: before I had time to think to myself, "What sort of performance will there be now?" my dear little animal began to make a row. And that was not all; he crawled out from under the bed, walked across the room, clattering his claws on the floor, waggling his ears, and suddenly collided with a chair which stood by the side of Vasíly Vasílitch's bed!

"Porfíry Kapítonitch,"—says Vasíly Vasílitch, and in such an indifferent voice, you know,—"I didn't know that thou hadst taken to keeping a dog. What sort of an animal is it—a setter?"

"I have no dog,"—said I,—"and I never have had one."

"Thou hast not indeed! But what's this?"

"What is this?"—said I.—"See here now; light the candle and thou wilt find out for thyself."

"It isn't a dog?"

"No."

Vasíly Vasílitch turned over in bed.—"But thou art jesting, damn it?"

"No, I'm not jesting."—I hear him go scratch, scratch with a match, and that thing does not stop, but scratches its side. The flame flashed up … and basta! There was not a trace of a dog! Vasíly Vasílitch stared at me—and I stared at him.

"What sort of a trick is this?"—said he.

"Why,"—said I,—"this is such a trick that if thou wert to set Socrates himself on one side and Frederick the Great on the other even they couldn't make head or tail of it."—And thereupon I told him all in detail. Up jumped my Vasíly Vasílitch as though he had been singed! He couldn't get into his boots.

"Horses!"—he yelled—"horses!"

I began to argue with him, but in vain. He simply groaned.

"I won't stay,"—he shouted,—"not a minute!—Of course, after this, thou art a doomed man!—Horses!…"

But I prevailed upon him. Only his bed was dragged out into another room—and night-lights were lighted everywhere. In the morning, at tea, he recovered his dignity; he began to give me advice.

"Thou shouldst try absenting thyself from the house for several days, Porfíry Kapítonitch," he said: "perhaps that vile thing would leave thee."

But I must tell you that he—that neighbour of mine—had a capacious mind! he worked his mother-in-law so famously among other things: he palmed off a note of hand on her, which signifies that he chose the most vulnerable moment! She became like silk: she gave him a power of attorney over all her property—what more would you have? But that was a great affair—to twist his mother-in-law round his finger—wasn't it, hey? Judge for yourselves. But he went away from me somewhat discontented; I had punished him to the extent of another hundred rubles. He even swore at me: "Thou art ungrateful,"—he said, "thou hast no feeling;" but how was I to blame for that? Well, this is in parenthesis—but I took his suggestion under consideration. That same day I drove off to town and established myself in an inn, with an acquaintance, an old man of the Old Ritualist sect.[2]

He was a worthy old man, although a trifle harsh, because of loneliness: his whole family were dead. Only he did not favour tobacco at all,[3] and felt a great loathing for dogs; I believe, for example, that rather than admit a dog into the room he would have rent himself in twain! "For how it is possible?"—he said. "There in my room, on the wall, the Sovereign Lady herself deigns to dwell;[4] and shall a filthy dog thrust his accursed snout in there?"—That was ignorance, of course! However, this is my opinion: if any man has been vouchsafed wisdom, let him hold to it!

"But you are a great philosopher, I see,"—interrupted Antón Stepánitch again, with the same laugh as before.

This time Porfíry Kapítonitch even scowled.

"What sort of a philosopher I am no one knows,"—he said as his moustache twitched in a surly manner:—"but I would gladly take you as a pupil."

We all fairly bored our eyes into Antón Stepánitch; each one of us expected an arrogant retort or at least a lightning glance.... But Mr. State Councillor altered his smile from scorn to indifference, then yawned, dangled his foot—and that was all!

So then, I settled down at that old man's house—[went on Porfíry Kapítonitch].—He assigned me a room "for acquaintance's" sake,—not of the best; he himself lodged there also, behind a partition—and that was all I required. But what tortures I did undergo! The chamber was small, it was hot, stifling, and there were flies, and such sticky ones; in the corner was a remarkably large case for images, with ancient holy pictures; their garments were dim and puffed out; the air was fairly infected with olive-oil, and some sort of a spice in addition; on the bedstead were two down beds; if you moved a pillow, outran a cockroach from beneath it.... I drank an incredible amount of tea, out of sheer tedium—it was simply horrible! I got into bed; it was impossible to sleep.—And on the other side of the partition my host was sighing and grunting and reciting his prayers. I heard him begin to snore—and very lightly and courteously, in old-fashioned style. I had long since extinguished my candle—only the shrine-lamp was twinkling in front of the holy pictures.... A hindrance, of course! So, I took and rose up softly, in my bare feet: I reached up to the lamp and blew it out.... Nothing happened.—"Aha!" I thought: "this means that he won't make a fuss in the house of strangers."... But no sooner had I lain down on the bed than the row began again! The thing clawed, and{336} scratched himself and flapped his ears ... well, just as I wanted him to. Good! I lay there and waited to see what would happen. I heard the old man wake up.

"Master,"—said he,—"hey there, master?"

"What's wanted?"—said I.

"Was it thou who didst put out the shrine-lamp?"—And without awaiting my reply, he suddenly began to mumble:

"What's that? What's that? A dog? A dog? Akh, thou damned Nikonian!"**[5]**

"Wait a bit, old man,"—said I,—"before thou cursest; but it would be better for thee to come hither thyself. Things deserving of wonder are going on here,"—said I.

The old man fussed about behind the partition and entered my room with a candle, a slender one, of yellow wax; and I was amazed as I looked at him! He was all bristling, with shaggy ears and vicious eyes like those of a polecat; on his head was a small skull-cap of white felt; his beard reached to his girdle and was white also; and he had on a waistcoat with brass buttons over his shirt, and fur boots on his feet, and he disseminated an odour of juniper. In that condition he went up to the holy pictures, crossed himself thrice with two fingers**[6]** lighted the shrine-lamp, crossed himself again, and turning to me, merely grunted:

"Explain thyself!"

Thereupon, without the least delay, I communicated to him all the circumstances. The old man listened to all my explanations without uttering the smallest word; he simply kept shaking his head. Then he sat down on my bed, still maintaining silence. He scratched his breast, the back of his head, and other places, and still remained silent.

"Well, Feodúl Ivánitch,"—said I, "what is thy opinion: is this some sort of visitation of the Evil One, thinkest thou?"

The old man stared at me.—"A pretty thing thou hast invented! A visitation of the Evil One, forsooth! 'Twould be all right at thy house, thou tobacco-user,—but 'tis quite another thing here! Only consider how many holy things there are here! And thou must needs have a visitation of the devil!—And if it isn't that what is it?"

The old man relapsed into silence, scratched himself again, and at last he said, but in a dull sort of way, because his moustache kept crawling into his mouth:

"Go thou to the town of Byéleff. There is only one man who can help thee. And that man dwells in Byéleff;**[7]** he is one of our people. If he takes a fancy to help thee, that's thy good luck; if he doesn't take a fancy,—so it must remain."

"But how am I to find him?"—said I.

"We can give thee directions,"—said he;—"only why dost thou call this a visitation of the devil? 'Tis a vision, or a sign; but thou wilt not be able to comprehend it; 'tis not within thy flight. And now lie down and sleep under Christ's protection, dear little father; I will fumigate with incense; and in the morning we will take counsel together. The morning is wiser than the evening, thou knowest."

Well, sir, and we did take counsel together in the morning—only I came near choking to death with that same incense. And the old man instructed me after this wise; that when I had reached Byéleff I was to go to the public square, and in the second shop on the right inquire for a certain Prokhóritch; and having found Prokhóritch, I was to hand him a document. And the whole document consisted of a scrap of paper, on which was written the following: "In the name of the Father, and of the Son, and of the Holy Spirit, Amen. To Sergyéi Prokhóritch Pervúshin. Trust this man. Feodúly Ivánovitch." And below: "Send some cabbages, for God's sake."

I thanked the old man, and without further ado ordered my tarantás to be harnessed and set off for Byéleff. For I argued in this way: admitting that my nocturnal visitor did not cause me much grief, still, nevertheless, it was not quite decorous for a nobleman and an officer—what do you think about it?

"And did you really go to Byéleff?"—whispered Mr. Finopléntoff.

I did, straight to Byéleff. I went to the square and inquired in the second shop on the right for Prokhóritch. "Is there such a man?"—I asked.

"There is,"—I was told.

"And where does he live?"

"On the Oká, beyond the vegetable-gardens."

"In whose house?"[8]

"His own."

I wended my way to the Oká, searched out his house, that is to say, not actually a house, but a downright hovel. I beheld a man in a patched blue overcoat and a tattered cap,—of the petty burgher class, judging by his appearance,—standing with his back to me, and digging in his cabbage-garden.—I went up to him.

"Are you such and such a one?"—said I.

He turned round,—and to tell you the truth, such piercing eyes I have never seen in all my life. But his whole face was no bigger than one's fist; his beard was wedge-shaped, and his lips were sunken: he was an aged man.

"I am he,"—he said.—"What do you wanta?"

"Why, here,"—said I;—"this is what I wanta,"—and I placed the document in his hand. He gazed at me very intently, and said:

"Please come into the house; I cannot read without my spectacles."

Well, sir, he and I went into his kennel—actually, a regular kennel; poor, bare, crooked; it barely held together. On the wall was a holy picture of ancient work,**[9]** as black as a coal; only the whites of the eyes were fairly burning in the faces of the holy people. He took some round iron spectacles from a small table, placed them on his nose, perused the writing, and through his spectacles again scrutinised me.

"You have need of me?"

"I have,"—said I,—"that's the fact."

"Well,"—said he, "if you have, then make your statement, and I will listen."

And just imagine; he sat down, and pulling a checked handkerchief from his pocket, he spread it out on his knees—and the handkerchief was full of holes—and gazed at me as solemnly as though he had been a senator,**[10]** or some minister or other; and did not ask me to sit down. And what was still more astonishing, I suddenly felt myself growing timid, so timid ... simply, my soul sank into my heels. He pierced me through and through with his eyes, and that's all there is to be said! But I recovered my self-possession and narrated to him my whole story. He remained silent for a while, shrank together, mowed with his lips, and then began to interrogate me, still as though he were a senator, so majestically and without haste. "What is your name?"—he asked. "How old are you? Who were your parents? Are you a bachelor or married?"—Then he began to mow with his lips again, frowned, thrust out his finger and said:

"Do reverence to the holy image of the honourable saints of Solovétzk,**[11]** Zósim and Savâty."

I made a reverence to the earth, and did not rise to my feet; such awe and submission did I feel for that man that I believe I would have instantly done anything whatsoever he might have ordered me!... I see that you are smiling, gentlemen; but I was in no mood for laughing then, by Heaven I was not.

"Rise, sir,"—he said at last.—"It is possible to help you. This has not been sent to you by way of punishment, but as a warning; it signifies that you are being looked after; someone is praying earnestly for you. Go now to the bazaar and buy yourself a bitch, which you must keep by you day and night, without ceasing. Your visions will cease, and your dog will prove necessary to you into the bargain."

A flash of light seemed suddenly to illuminate me; how those words did please me! I made obeisance to Prokhóritch, and was on the point of departing, but remembered that it was impossible for me not to show him my gratitude; I drew a three-ruble note from my pocket. But he put aside my hand and said to me:

"Give it to our chapel, or to the poor, for this service is gratis."

Again, I made him an obeisance, nearly to the girdle, and immediately marched off to the bazaar. And fancy, no sooner had I begun to approach the shops when behold, a man in a frieze cloak advanced to meet me, and under his arm he carried a setter bitch, two months old, with light-brown hair, a white muzzle, and white fore paws.

"Halt!" said I to the man in the frieze cloak; "what will you take for her?"

"Two rubles in silver."

"Take three!"

The man was astonished, and thought the gentleman had lost his mind—but I threw a banknote in his teeth, seized the bitch in my arms and rushed to my tarantás. The coachman harnessed up the horses briskly, and that same evening I was at home. The dog sat on my lap during the whole journey—and never uttered a sound; but I kept saying to her: "Tresórushko! Tresórushko!" I immediately gave her food and water, ordered straw to be brought, put her to bed, and dashed into bed myself. I blew out the light; darkness reigned.

"Come now, begin!"—said I.—Silence.—"Do begin, thou thus and so!"—Not a sound. It was laughable. I began to take courage.—"Come now, begin, thou thus and so, and 'tother thing!" But nothing happened—there was a complete lull! The only thing to be heard was the bitch breathing hard.

"Fílka!"—I shouted;—"Fílka! Come hither, stupid man!"—He entered.—"Dost thou hear the dog?"

"No, master,"—said he,—"I don't hear anything,"—and began to laugh.

"And thou wilt not hear it again forever! Here's half a ruble for thee for vodka!"

"Please let me kiss your hand,"—said the fool, and crawled to me in the dark.... My joy was great, I can tell you!

"And was that the end of it all?"—asked Antón Stepánitch, no longer ironically.

The visions did cease, it is true—and there were no disturbances of any sort—but wait, that was not the end of the whole matter. My Tresórushko began to grow and turned out a cunning rogue. Thick-tailed, heavy, flop-eared, with drooping dewlaps, she was a regular "take-advance,"—a thoroughgoing good setter. And moreover, she became greatly attached to me. Hunting is bad in our parts,—well, but as I had set up a dog I had to supply myself with a gun also. I began to roam about the surrounding country with my Tresór; sometimes I would knock over a hare (my heavens, how she did course those hares!), and sometimes a quail or a duck. But the chief point was that Tresór never, never strayed a step away from me. Wherever I went, there she went also; I even took her to the bath with me—truly! One of our young gentlewomen undertook to eject me from her drawing-room on account of Tresór; but I raised such a row that I smashed some of her window-panes!

Well, sir, one day—it happened in summer.... And I must tell you that there was such a drought that no one could recall it's like; the air was full of something which was neither smoke nor fog; there was an odour of burning, and mist, and the sun was like a red-hot cannon-ball; and the dust was such that one could not leave off sneezing! People went about with their mouths gaping open, just like crows.

It bored me to sit at home constantly in complete undress, behind closed shutters; and by the way, the heat was beginning to moderate.... And so, gentlemen, I set off afoot to the house of one of my neighbours. This neighbour of mine lived about a verst from me,—

and was really a benevolent lady. She was still young and blooming, and of the most attractive exterior; only she had a fickle disposition. But that is no detriment in the feminine sex; it even affords pleasure.... So, then, I trudged to her porch—and that trip seemed very salt to me! Well, I thought, Nimfodóra Semyónovna will regale me with bilberry-water, and other refreshments—and I had already grasped the door-handle when, suddenly, around the corner of the servants' cottage there arose a trampling of feet, a squealing and shouting of small boys.... I looked round. O Lord, my God! Straight toward me was dashing a huge, reddish beast, which at first sight I did not recognise as a dog; its jaws were gaping, its eyes were blood-shot, its hair stood on end.... Before I could take breath the monster leaped upon the porch, elevated itself on its hind legs, and fell straight on my breast. What do you think of that situation? I was swooning with fright and could not lift my arms; I was completely stupefied; ... all I could see were the white tusks right at the end of my nose, the red tongue all swathed in foam. But at that moment another dark body soared through the air in front of me, like a ball—it was my darling Tresór coming to my rescue; and she went at that beast's throat like a leech! The beast rattled hoarsely in the throat, gnashed its teeth, staggered back.... With one jerk I tore open the door and found myself in the anteroom. I stood there, beside myself with terror, threw my whole body against the lock, and listened to a desperate battle which was in progress on the porch. I began to shout, to call for help; everyone in the house took alarm. Nimfodóra Semyónovna ran up with hair unbraided; voices clamoured in the courtyard—and suddenly there came a cry; "Hold him, hold him, lock the gate!"

I opened the door,—just a crack,—and looked. The monster was no longer on the porch. People were rushing in disorder about the courtyard, flourishing their arms, picking up billets of wood from the ground—just as though they had gone mad. "To the village! It has run to the village!" shrieked shrilly a peasant-woman in a pointed coronet head-dress of unusual dimensions, thrusting her head through a garret-window. I emerged from the house.

"Where is Tresór?"—said I.—And at that moment I caught sight of my saviour. She was walking away from the gate, limping, all bitten, and covered with blood....

"But what was it, after all?"—I asked the people, as they went circling round the courtyard like crazy folk.

"A mad dog!"—they answered me, "belonging to the Count; it has been roving about here since yesterday."

We had a neighbour, a Count; he had introduced some very dreadful dogs from oversea. My knees gave way beneath me; I hastened to the mirror and looked to see whether I had been bitten. No; God be thanked, nothing was visible; only, naturally, my face was all green; but Nimfodóra Semyónovna was lying on the couch and clucking like a hen. And that was easily to be understood: in the first place, nerves; in the second place, sensibility. But she came to herself, and asked me in a very languid way: was I alive? I told her that I was, and that Tresór was my saviour.

"Akh,"—said she,—"what nobility! And I suppose the mad dog smothered her?"

"No,"—said I,—"it did not smother her, but it wounded her seriously."

"Akh,"—said she,—"in that case, she must be shot this very moment!"

"Nothing of the sort,"—said I;—"I won't agree to that; I shall try to cure her." ...

In the meanwhile, Tresór began to scratch at the door; I started to open it for her.

"Akh,"—cried she,—"what are you doing? Why, she will bite us all dreadfully!"

"Pardon me,"—said I,—"the poison does not take effect so soon."

"Akh,"—said she,—"how is that possible? Why, you have gone out of your mind!"

"Nimfótchka,"—said I,—"calm thyself; listen to reason...."

But all at once she began to scream: "Go away; go away this instant with your disgusting dog!"

"I will go,"—said I.

"Instantly,"—said she,—"this very second! Take thyself off, brigand,"—said she,—"and don't dare ever to show yourself in my sight again. Thou mightest go mad thyself!"

"Very good, ma'am,"—said I; "only give me an equipage, for I am afraid to go home on foot now."

She riveted her eyes on me. "Give, give him a calash, a carriage, a drozhky, whatever he wants,—anything, for the sake of getting rid of him as quickly as possible. Akh, what eyes! akh, what eyes he has!"—And with these words she flew out of the room, dealing a maid who was entering a box on the ear,—and I heard her go off into another fit of hysterics.—And you may believe me or not, gentlemen, but from that day forth I broke off all acquaintance with Nimfodóra Semyónovna; and, taking all things into mature consideration, I cannot but add that for that circumstance also I owe my friend Tresór a debt of gratitude until I lie down in my coffin.

Well, sir, I ordered a calash to be harnessed, placed Tresór in it, and drove off home with her. At home I looked her over, washed her wounds, and thought to myself: "I'll take her tomorrow, as soon as it is light, to the wizard in Efrém County. Now this wizard was an old peasant, a wonderful man; he would whisper over water—but others say that he emitted serpents' venom on it—and give it to you to drink, and your malady would instantly disappear. By the way, I thought, I'll get myself bled in Efrémovo; 'tis a good remedy for terror; only, of course, not from the arm, but from the bleeding-vein."

"But where is that place—the bleeding-vein?"—inquired Finopléntoff, with bashful curiosity.

Don't you know? That spot on the fist close to the thumb, on which one shakes snuff from the horn.—Just here, see! 'Tis the very best place for blood-letting; therefore, judge for yourselves; from the arm it will be venal blood, while from this spot it is sparkling. The doctors don't know that, and don't understand it; how should they, the sluggards, the dumb idiots? Blacksmiths chiefly make use of it. And what skillful fellows they are! They'll place their chisel on the spot, give it a whack with their hammer—and the deed is done!... Well, sir, while I was meditating in this wise, it had grown entirely dark out of doors, and it was time to go to sleep. I lay down on my bed, and Tresór, of course, was there also. But whether it was because of my fright or of the stifling heat, or because the fleas or my thoughts were bothersome, at any rate, I could not get to sleep. Such distress fell upon me as it is impossible to describe; and I kept drinking water, and opening the window, and thrumming the "Kamárynskaya"**[12]** on the guitar, with Italian variations.... In vain! I felt impelled to leave the room,—and that's all there was to it. At last, I made up my mind. I took a pillow, a coverlet, and a sheet, and wended my way across the garden to the hay-barn; well, and there I settled myself. And there things were agreeable to me, gentlemen; the night was still, extremely still, only now and then a breeze as soft as a woman's hand would blow across my cheek, and it was very cool; the hay was fragrant as tea, the katydids were rasping in the apple-trees; then suddenly a quail would emit its call—and you would feel that he was taking his ease, the scamp, sitting in the dew with his mate.... And the sky was so magnificent; the stars were twinkling, and sometimes a little cloud, as white as the wadding, would float past, and even it would hardly stir....

At this point in the narrative, Skvorévitch sneezed; Kinarévitch, who never lagged behind his comrade in anything, sneezed also. Antón Stepánitch cast a glance of approbation at both.

Well, sir—[went on Porfíry Kapítonitch],—so I lay there and still, I could not get to sleep. A fit of meditation had seized upon me; and I pondered chiefly over the great marvel, how that Prokhóritch had rightly explained to me about the warning—and why such wonders should happen to me in particular.... I was astonished, in fact, because I could not understand it at all—while Tresórushko whimpered as she curled herself up on the hay; her wounds were paining her. And I'll tell you another thing that kept me from sleeping—you will hardly believe it, the moon! It stood right in front of me, so round and big and yellow and flat; and it seemed to me as though it were staring at me—by Heaven it did; and so arrogantly, importunately.... At last, I stuck my tongue out at it, I really did. Come, I thought, what art thou so curious about? I turned away from it; but it crawled into my ear, it illuminated the back of my head, and flooded me as though with rain; I opened my eyes, and what did I see? It made every blade of grass, every little wretched blade in the hay, the most insignificant spider's web, stand out distinctly! "Well, look, then!" said I. There was no help for it. I propped my head on my hand and began to stare at it. But I could not keep it up; if you will believe it, my eyes began to stick out like a hare's and to open very wide indeed, just as though they did not know what sleep was like. I think I could have eaten up everything with those same eyes. The gate of the hay-barn stood wide open; I could see for a distance of five versts out on the plain; and distinctly, not in the usual way on a moonlight night. So, I gazed and gazed and did not even wink.... And suddenly it seemed to me as though something were waving about far, far away ... exactly as though things were glimmering indistinctly before my eyes. Some time elapsed; again, a shadow leaped across my vision,—a little nearer now; then again, still nearer. What is it? I thought. Can it be a hare? No, I thought, it is larger than a hare, and its gait is unlike that of a hare. I continued to look, and again the shadow showed itself, and it was moving now across the pasture-land (and the pasture-land was whitish from the moonlight) like a very large spot; it was plain that it was some sort of a wild beast—a fox or a wolf. My heart contracted within me ... but what was I afraid of, after all? Aren't there plenty of wild animals running about the fields by night? But my curiosity was stronger than my fears; I rose up, opened my eyes very wide, and suddenly turned cold all over. I fairly froze rigidly on the spot, as though I had been buried in ice up to my ears; and why? The Lord only knows! And I saw the shadow growing bigger and bigger, which meant that it was making straight for the hay-barn.... And then it became apparent to me that it really was a large, big-headed wild beast.... It dashed onward like a whirlwind, like a bullet.... Good heavens! What was it? Suddenly it stopped short, as though it scented something.... Why, it was the mad dog I had encountered that day! 'Twas he, 'twas he! O Lord! And I could not stir a finger, I could not shout.... It ran to the gate, glared about with its eyes, emitted a howl, and dashed straight for me on the hay!

But out of the hay, like a lion, sprang my Tresór; and then the struggle began. The two clinched jaw to jaw and rolled over the ground in a ball! What took place further I do not remember; all I do remember is that I flew head over heels across them, just as I was, into the garden, into the house, and into my own bedroom!... I almost dived under the bed—there's no use in concealing the fact. And what leaps, what bounds I made in the garden! You would have taken me for the leading ballerina who dances before the Emperor Napoleon on the day of his Angel—and even she couldn't have overtaken me. But when I had recovered myself a little, I immediately routed out the entire household; I ordered them all to arm themselves, and I myself took a sword and a revolver. (I must confess that I had purchased that revolver after the Emancipation, in case of need, you know—only I had hit upon such a beast of a pedlar that out of three charges two inevitably missed fire.) Well, sir, I took all this, and in this guise we sallied forth, in a regular horde, with staves and lanterns, and directed our footsteps toward the hay-barn. We reached it and called—nothing was to be heard; we entered the barn at last.... and what did we see? My poor Tresórushko lay dead, with her throat slit, and that accursed beast had vanished without leaving a trace!

Then, gentlemen, I began to bleat like a calf, and I will say it without shame; I fell down on the body of my twofold rescuer, so to speak, and kissed her head for a long time. And there I remained in that attitude until my old housekeeper, Praskóvya, brought me to my senses (she also had run out at the uproar).

"Why do you grieve so over the dog, Porfíry Stepánitch?"—said she. "You will surely catch cold, which God forbid!" (I was very lightly clad.) "And if that dog lost her life in saving you, she ought to reckon it as a great favour!"

Although I did not agree with Praskóvya, I went back to the house. And the mad dog was shot on the following day by a soldier from the garrison. And it must have been that that was the end appointed by Fate to the dog, for the soldier fired a gun for the first time in his life, although he had a medal for service in the year '12. So that is the supernatural occurrence which happened to me.

The narrator ceased speaking and began to fill his pipe. But we all exchanged glances of surprise.

"But perhaps you lead a very upright life,"—began Mr. Finopléntoff,—"and so by way of reward...." But at that word he faltered, for he saw that Porfíry Kapítonitch's cheeks were beginning to swell out and turn red, and his eyes too were beginning to pucker up—evidently the man was on the point of breaking out....

"But admitting the possibility of the supernatural, the possibility of its interference in everyday life, so to speak,"—began Antón Stepánitch:—"then what rôle, after this, must sound sense play?"

None of us found any answer, and, as before, we remained perplexed.

FOOTNOTES:

[1] The fifth (from the top) of the fourteen grades in the Table of Ranks, instituted by Peter the Great, which were to be won by service to the State.—Translator.

[2] Those who reject the official and necessary corrections made in the Scriptures and Church service books in the reign of Peter the Great's father.—Translator.

[3] The Old Ritualists oppose tea, coffee, and tobacco, chiefly, it would seem, because they are "newfangled," having come into use after the schism. Later on, they invented curious religious reasons for their denunciation of these and other things.—Translator.

[4] The holy picture (*ikóna*) of the Mother of Christ.—Translator.

[5] The Old Ritualists' most opprobrious epithet, designating a member of the State Church, which accepted the emendations instituted by Patriarch Níkon referred to in a previous note.—Translator.

[6] One of the hotly disputed points of difference between the Old Ritualists and the members of the State Church is in their manner of crossing themselves. The latter use the forefinger, middle finger, and thumb joined at the tips.—Translator.

[7] In the government of Tula, central Russia.—Translator.

[8] Formerly, houses were not numbered, and addresses ran: "In the house of ***" (the proprietor, man or woman), often with many complicated directions added to designate the special house. These

ancient addresses still remain, along with the numbers or alone, especially on many of the houses in Moscow, and in country towns.—Translator.

[9] Old Ritualists will tolerate no others. Neither will they employ the words "buy" or "sell" in connection with these ikónas; they say "exchange."—Translator.

[10] The Senate in Russia is the Supreme Court of Appeals, and the senators are appointed, not elected.—Translator.

[11] A famous monastery on an island in the White Sea.—Translator.

[12] A vivacious and favourite popular dance-tune. It is several centuries old, and of interesting historical origin.—Translator.

THE DISTRICT DOCTOR

One day in autumn on my way back from a remote part of the country I caught a cold and fell ill. Fortunately, the fever attacked me in the district town at the inn; I sent for the doctor. In half-an-hour the district doctor appeared, a thin, dark-haired man of middle height. He prescribed me the usual sudorific, ordered a mustard-plaster to be put on, very deftly slid a five-ruble note up his sleeve, coughing drily and looking away as he did so, and then was getting up to go home, but somehow fell into talk and remained. I was exhausted with feverishness; I foresaw a sleepless night and was glad of a little chat with a pleasant companion. Tea was served. My doctor began to converse freely. He was a sensible fellow and expressed himself with vigour and some humour. Queer things happen in the world: you may live a long while with some people, and be on friendly terms with them, and never once speak openly with them from your soul; with others you have scarcely time to get acquainted, and all at once you are pouring out to him—or he to you—all your secrets, as though you were at confession. I don't know how I gained the confidence of my new friend—anyway, with nothing to lead up to it, he told me a rather curious incident; and here I will report his tale for the information of the indulgent reader. I will try to tell it in the doctor's own words.

"You don't happen to know," he began in a weak and quavering voice (the common result of the use of unmixed Berezov snuff); "you don't happen to know the judge here, Mylov, Pavel Lukich?... You don't know him?... Well, it's all the same." (He cleared his throat and rubbed his eyes.) "Well, you see, the thing happened, to tell you exactly without mistake, in Lent, at the very time of the thaws. I was sitting at his house—our judge's, you know—playing preference. Our judge is a good fellow, and fond of playing preference. Suddenly" (the doctor made frequent use of this word, suddenly) "they tell me, 'There's a servant asking for you.' I say, 'What does he want?' They say, "He has brought a note—it must be from a patient.' 'Give me the note,' I say. So, it is from a patient—well and good—you understand—it's our bread and butter... But this is how it was: a lady, a widow, writes to me; she says, 'My daughter is dying. Come, for God's sake!' she says, 'and the horses have been sent for you.'... Well, that's all right. But she was twenty miles from the town, and it was midnight out of doors, and the roads in such a state, my word! And as she was poor herself, one could not expect more than two silver rubles, and even that problematic; and perhaps it might only be a matter of a roll of linen and a sack of oatmeal in *payment*. However, duty, you know, before everything: a fellow-creature may be dying. I hand over my cards at once to Kalliopin, the member of the provincial commission, and return home. I look; a wretched little trap was standing at the steps, with peasant's horses, fat—too fat—and their coat as shaggy as felt; and the coachman sitting with his cap off out of respect. Well, I think to myself, 'It's clear, my friend, these patients aren't rolling in riches.'... You smile; but I tell you, a poor man like me has to take everything into consideration... If the coachman sits like a prince, and doesn't touch his cap, and even sneers at you behind his beard, and flicks his whip—then you may bet on six rubles. But this case, I saw, had a very different air. However, I think there's no help for it; duty before everything. I snatch up the most necessary drugs and set off. Will you believe it? I only managed to get there at all. The road was infernal: streams, snow, watercourses, and the dyke had suddenly burst there—that was the worst of it! However, I arrived at last. It was a little thatched house. There was a light in the windows; that meant they expected me. I was met by an old lady, very venerable, in a cap. 'Save her!' she says; 'she is dying.' I say, 'Pray don't distress yourself—Where is the invalid?' 'Come this way.' I see a clean little room, a lamp in the corner; on the bed a girl of twenty, unconscious. She was in a burning heat and breathing heavily—it was fever. There were two other girls, her sisters, scared and in tears. 'Yesterday,' they tell me, 'she was perfectly well and had a good appetite; this morning she complained of her head, and this evening, suddenly, you see, like this.' I say again: 'Pray don't be uneasy.' It's a doctor's duty, you know—and

I went up to her and bled her, told them to put on a mustard-plaster, and prescribed a mixture. Meantime I looked at her; I looked at her, you know—there, by God! I had never seen such a face!—she was a beauty, in a word! I felt quite shaken with pity. Such lovely features; such eyes!... But thank God! she became easier; she fell into a perspiration, seemed to come to her senses, looked round, smiled, and passed her hand over her face... Her sisters bent over her. They ask, 'How are you?' 'All right,' she says, and turns away. I looked at her; she had fallen asleep. 'Well,' I say, 'now the patient should be left alone.' So, we all went out on tiptoe; only a maid remained, in case she was wanted. In the parlour there was a samovar standing on the table, and a bottle of rum; in our profession one can't get on without it. They gave me tea; they asked me to stop the night... I consented: where could I go, indeed, at that time of night? The old lady kept groaning. 'What is it?' I say, 'she will live; don't worry yourself; you had better take a little rest yourself; it is about two o'clock.' 'But will you send to wake me if anything happens?' 'Yes, yes.' The old lady went away, and the girls too went to their own room; they made up a bed for me in the parlour. Well, I went to bed—but I could not get to sleep, for a wonder! Because in reality I was very tired. I could not get my patient out of my head. At last, I could not put up with it any longer; I got up suddenly; I think to myself, 'I will go and see how the patient is getting on.' Her bedroom was next to the parlour. Well, I got up, and gently opened the door—how my heartbeat! I looked in: the servant was asleep, her mouth wide open, and even snoring, the wretch! but the patient lay with her face towards me and her arms flung wide apart, poor girl! I went up to her ... when suddenly she opened her eyes and stared at me! 'Who is it? who is it?' I was in confusion. 'Don't be alarmed, madam,' I say; 'I am the doctor; I have come to see how you feel.' 'You the doctor?' 'Yes, the doctor; your mother sent for me from the town; we have bled you, madam; now pray go to sleep, and in a day or two, please God! we will set you on your feet again.' 'Ah, yes, yes, doctor, don't let me die... please, please.' 'Why do you talk like that? God bless you!' She is in a fever again, I think to myself; I felt her pulse; yes, she was feverish. She looked at me, and then took me by the hand. 'I will tell you why I don't want to die: I will tell you... Now we are alone; and only, please don't you ... not to anyone ... Listen...'

I bent down; she moved her lips quite to my ear; she touched my cheek with her hair—I confess my head went round—and began to whisper... I could make out nothing of it... Ah, she was delirious! ... She whispered and whispered, but so quickly, and as if it were not in Russian; at last, she finished and shivering dropped her head on the pillow, and threatened me with her finger: 'Remember, doctor, to no one.' I calmed her somehow, gave her something to drink, woke the servant, and went away."

At this point the doctor again took snuff with exasperated energy, and for a moment seemed stupefied by its effects.

"However," he continued, "the next day, contrary to my expectations, the patient was no better. I thought and thought, and suddenly decided to remain there, even though my other patients were expecting me... And you know one can't afford to disregard that; one's practice suffers if one does. But, in the first place, the patient was really in danger; and secondly, to tell the truth, I felt strongly drawn to her. Besides, I liked the whole family. Though they were really badly off, they were singularly, I may say, cultivated people... Their father had been a learned man, an author; he died, of course, in poverty, but he had managed before he died to give his children an excellent education; he left a lot of books too. Either because I looked after the invalid very carefully, or for some other reason; anyway, I can venture to say all the household loved me as if I were one of the family... Meantime the roads were in a worse state than ever; all communications, so to say, were cut off completely; even medicine could with difficulty be got from the town... The sick girl was not getting better... Day after day, and day after day ... but ... here..." (The doctor made a brief pause.) "I declare I don't know how to tell you."... (He again took snuff, coughed, and swallowed a little tea.) "I will tell you without beating about the bush. My patient ... how should I say?... Well, she had fallen in love with me ... or, no, it was not that she was in love ... however ... really, how should one say?" (The doctor looked down and grew red.) "No," he went on quickly, "in love, indeed! A man should not over-estimate himself. She was an educated girl, clever and well-read, and I had even forgotten my Latin, one may say, completely. As to appearance" (the doctor looked himself over with a smile) "I am nothing to boast of there either. But God Almighty did not make me a fool; I don't take black for white; I know a thing or two; I could see very clearly, for instance that Aleksandra Andreyevna—that was her name—did not feel love for me, but had a friendly, so to say, inclination—a respect or something for me. Though she herself perhaps mistook this sentiment, anyway this was her attitude; you may form your own judgment of it. But" added the doctor, who had brought out all these disconnected sentences without taking breath, and with obvious embarrassment, "I seem to be wandering rather—you won't understand anything like this ... There, with your leave, I will relate it all in order."

He drank off a glass of tea and began in a calmer voice.

"Well, then. My patient kept getting worse and worse. You are not a doctor, my good sir; you cannot understand what passes in a poor fellow's heart, especially at first, when he begins to suspect that the disease is getting the upper hand of him. What becomes of his belief in himself? You suddenly grow so timid; it's indescribable. You fancy then that you have forgotten everything you knew, and that the patient has no faith in you, and that other people begin to notice how distracted you are and tell you the symptoms with reluctance; that they are looking at you suspiciously, whispering... Ah! it's horrid! There must be a remedy, you think, for this disease, if one could find it. Isn't this it? You try—no, that's not it! You don't allow the medicine the necessary time to do good... You clutch at one thing, then at another. Sometimes you take up a book of medical prescriptions—here it is, you think! Sometimes, by Jove, you pick one out by chance, thinking to leave it to fate... But meantime a fellow-creature's dying, and another doctor would have saved him. 'We must have a consultation,' you say; 'I will not take the responsibility on myself.' And what a fool you look at such times! Well, in time you learn to bear it; it's nothing to you. A man has died—but it's not your fault; you treated him by the rules. But what's still more torture to you is to see blind faith in you, and to feel yourself that you are not able to be of use. Well, it was just this blind faith that the whole of Aleksandra Andreyevna's family had in me; they had forgotten to think that their daughter was in danger. I, too, on my side assure them that it's nothing, but meantime my heart sinks into my boots. To add to our troubles, the roads were in such a state that the coachman was gone for whole days together to get medicine. And I never left the patient's room; I could not tear myself away; I tell her amusing stories, you know, and play cards with her. I watch by her side at night. The old mother thanks me with tears in her eyes; but I think to myself, 'I don't deserve your gratitude.' I frankly confess to you—there is no object in concealing it now—I was in love with my patient. And Aleksandra Andreyevna had grown fond of me; she would sometimes not let anyone be in her room but me. She began to talk to me, to ask me questions; where I had studied, how I lived, who are my people, whom I go to see. I feel that she ought not to talk; but to forbid her to—to forbid her resolutely, you know—I could not. Sometimes I held my head in my hands, and asked myself, "What are you doing, villain?"... And she would take my hand and hold it, give me a long, long look, and turn away, sigh, and say, 'How good you are!' Her hands were so feverish, her eyes so large and languid... 'Yes,' she says, 'you are a good, kind man; you are not like our neighbours... No, you are not like that... Why did I not know you till now!' 'Aleksandra Andreyevna, calm yourself,' I say... 'I feel, believe me, I don't know how I have gained ... but there, calm yourself... All will be right; you will be well again.' And meanwhile I must tell you," continued the doctor, bending forward and raising his eyebrows, "that they associated very little with the neighbours, because the smaller people were not on their level, and pride hindered them from being friendly with the rich. I tell you; they were an exceptionally cultivated family; so, you know it was gratifying for me. She would only take her medicine from my hands ... she would lift herself up, poor girl, with my aid, take it, and gaze at me... My heart felt as if it were bursting. And meanwhile she was growing worse and worse, worse and worse, all the time; she will die, I think to myself; she must die. Believe me, I would sooner have gone to the grave myself; and here were her mother and sisters watching me, looking into my eyes ... and their faith in me was wearing away. 'Well? how is she?' 'Oh, all right, all right!' All right, indeed! My mind was failing me. Well, I was sitting one night alone again by my patient. The maid was sitting there too and snoring away in full swing; I can't find fault with the poor girl, though; she was worn out too. Aleksandra Andreyevna had felt very unwell all the evening; she was very feverish. Until midnight she kept tossing about; at last, she seemed to fall asleep; at least, she lay still without stirring. The lamp was burning in the corner before the holy image. I sat there, you know, with my head bent; I even dozed a little. Suddenly it seemed as though some one touched me in the side; I turned round... Good God! Aleksandra Andreyevna was gazing with intent eyes at me ... her lips parted, her cheeks seemed burning. 'What is it?' 'Doctor, shall I die?' 'Merciful Heavens!' 'No, doctor, no; please don't tell me I shall live ... don't say so... If you knew... Listen! for God's sake don't conceal my real position,' and her breath came so fast. 'If I can know for certain that I must die ... then I will tell you all— all!' 'Aleksandra Andreyevna, I beg!' 'Listen; I have not been asleep at all ... I have been looking at you a long while... For God's sake!... I believe in you; you are a good man, an honest man; I entreat you by all that is sacred in the world—tell me the truth! If you knew how important it is for me... Doctor, for God's sake tell me... Am I in danger?' 'What can I tell you, Aleksandra Andreyevna, pray?' 'For God's sake, I beseech you!' 'I can't disguise from you,' I say, 'Aleksandra Andreyevna; you are certainly in danger; but God is merciful.' 'I shall die, I shall die.' And it seemed as though she were pleased; her face grew so bright; I was alarmed. 'Don't be afraid, don't be afraid! I am not frightened of death at all.' She suddenly sat up and leaned on her elbow. 'Now ... yes, now I can tell you that I thank you with my whole heart ... that you are kind and good—that I love you!' I stare at her, like one possessed; it was terrible for me, you know. 'Do you hear, I love you!' 'Aleksandra Andreyevna, how have I deserved—' 'No, no, you don't—you don't understand me.'... And suddenly she stretched out her arms, and taking my head in her hands, she kissed it... Believe me, I almost screamed aloud... I threw myself on my knees and buried my head in the pillow. She did not speak; her fingers trembled in my hair; I listen; she is weeping. I began to soothe her, to assure her... I really don't know what I did say to her. 'You will wake up the girl,' I say to her; 'Aleksandra Andreyevna, I thank you ... believe me ... calm yourself.' 'Enough, enough!' she persisted; 'never mind all of them; let them wake, then; let them come in—it does not matter; I am dying, you see... And what do you fear? why are you afraid? Lift up your head... Or, perhaps, you don't love me; perhaps I am wrong... In that case, forgive me.'

'Aleksandra Andreyevna, what are you saying!... I love you, Aleksandra Andreyevna.' She looked straight into my eyes and opened her arms wide. 'Then take me in your arms.' I tell you frankly, I don't know how it was I did not go mad that night. I feel that my patient is killing herself; I see that she is not fully herself; I understand, too, that if she did not consider herself on the point of death, she would never have thought of me; and, indeed, say what you will, it's hard to die at twenty without having known love; this was what was torturing her; this was why, in despair, she caught at me—do you understand now? But she held me in her arms and would not let me go. 'Have pity on me, Aleksandra Andreyevna, and have pity on yourself,' I say. 'Why,' she says; 'what is there to think of? You know I must die.' ... This she repeated incessantly ... 'If I knew that I should return to life, and be a proper young lady again, I would be ashamed ... of course, ashamed ... but why now?' 'But who has said you will die?' 'Oh, no, leave off! you will not deceive me; you don't know how to lie—look at your face.' ... 'You shall live, Aleksandra Andreyevna; I will cure you; we will ask your mother's blessing ... we will be united—we will be happy.' 'No, no, I have your word; I must die ... you have promised me ... you have told me.' ... It was cruel for me—cruel for many reasons. And see what trifling things can do sometimes; it seems nothing at all, but it's painful. It occurred to her to ask me what my name is; not my surname, but my first name. I must be so unlucky as to be called Trifon. Yes, indeed; Trifon Ivanich. Everyone in the house called me to see a doctor. However, there's no help for it. I say, 'Trifon, madam.' She frowned, shook her head, and muttered something in French—ah, something unpleasant, of course!—and then she laughed—disagreeably too. Well, I spent the whole night with her in this way. Before morning I went away, feeling as though I were mad. When I went again into her room it was daytime, after morning tea. Good God! I could scarcely recognise her; people are laid in their grave looking better than that. I swear to you, on my honour, I don't understand—I absolutely don't understand—now, how I lived through that experience. Three days and nights my patient still lingered on. And what nights! What things she said to me! And on the last night—only imagine to yourself—I was sitting near her and kept praying to God for one thing only: 'Take her,' I said, 'quickly, and me with her.' Suddenly the old mother comes unexpectedly into the room. I had already the evening before told her—-the mother—there was little hope, and it would be well to send for a priest. When the sick girl saw her mother she said: 'It's very well you have come; look at us, we love one another—we have given each other our word.' 'What does she say, doctor?" What does she say?' I turned livid. 'She *is* wandering,' I say; 'the fever.' But she: 'Hush, hush; you told me something quite different just now, and have taken my ring. Why do you pretend? My mother is good—she will forgive—she will understand—and I am dying. ... I have no need to tell lies; give me your hand.' I jumped up and ran out of the room. The old lady, of course, guessed how it was.

"I will not, however, weary you any longer, and to me too, of course, it's painful to recall all this. My patient passed away the next day. God rest her soul!" the doctor added, speaking quickly and with a sigh. "Before her death she asked her family to go out and leave me alone with her."

"'Forgive me,' she said; 'I am perhaps to blame towards you ... my illness ... but believe me, I have loved no one more than you ... do not forget me ... keep my ring.'"

The doctor turned away; I took his hand.

"Ah!" he said, "let us talk of something else, or would you care to play preference for a small stake? It is not for people like me to give way to exalted emotions. There's only one thing for me to think of; how to keep the children from crying and the wife from scolding. Since then, you know, I have had time to enter into lawful wedlock, as they say... Oh ... I took a merchant's daughter—seven thousand for her dowry. Her name's Akulina; it goes well with Trifon. She is an ill-tempered woman, I must tell you, but luckily she's asleep all day... Well, shall it be preference?"

We sat down to preference for half-penny points. Trifon Ivanich won two rubles and a half from me, and went home late, well pleased with his success.

ENOUGH

A FRAGMENT FROM THE NOTE-BOOK OF A DEAD ARTIST

I

II

III

'Enough,' I said to myself as I moved with lagging steps over the steep mountainside down to the quiet little brook. 'Enough,' I said again, as I drank in the resinous fragrance of the pinewood, strong and pungent in the freshness of falling evening. 'Enough,' I said once more, as I sat on the mossy mound above the little brook and gazed into its dark, lingering waters, over which the sturdy reeds thrust up their pale green blades.... 'Enough.'

No more struggle, no more strain, time to draw in, time to keep firm hold of the head and to bid the heart be silent. No more to brood over the voluptuous sweetness of vague, seductive ecstasy, no more to run after each fresh form of beauty, no more to hang over every tremour of her delicate, strong wings.

All has been felt, all has been gone through... I am weary. What to me now that at this moment, larger, fiercer than ever, the sunset floods the heavens as though aflame with some triumphant passion? What to me that, amid the soft peace and glow of evening, suddenly, two paces hence, hidden in a thick bush's dewy stillness, a nightingale has sung his heart out in notes magical as though no nightingale had been on earth before him, and he first sang the first song of first love? All this was, has been, has been again, and is a thousand times repeated—and to think that it will last on so to all eternity—as though decreed, ordained—it stirs one's wrath! Yes... wrath!

IV

Ah, I am grown old! Such thoughts would never have come to me once—in those happy days of old, when I too was aflame like the sunset and my heart sang like the nightingale.

There is no hiding it—everything has faded about me, all life has paled. The light that gives life's colours depth and meaning—the light that comes out of the heart of man—is dead within me.... No, not dead yet—it feebly smoulders on, giving no light, no warmth.

Once, late in the night in Moscow, I remember I went up to the grating window of an old church and leaned against the faulty pane. It was dark under the low arched roof—a forgotten lamp shed a dull red light upon the ancient picture; dimly could be discerned the lips only of the sacred face—stern and sorrowful. The sullen darkness gathered about it; ready it seemed to crush under its dead weight the feeble ray of impotent light.... Such now in my heart is the light and such darkness.

V

And this I write to thee, to thee, my one never forgotten friend, to thee, my dear companion, whom I have left for ever, but shall not cease to love till my life's end.... Alas! thou knowest what parted us. But that I have no wish to speak of now. I have left thee... but even here, in these wilds, in this far off exile, I am all filled through and through with thee; as of old I am in thy power, as of old I feel the sweet burden of thy hand on my bent head!

For the last time I drag myself from out the grave of silence in which I am lying now. I turn a brief and softened gaze on all my past... our past.... No hope and no return; but no bitterness is in my heart and no regret, and clearer than the blue of heaven, purer than the first snow on mountain tops, fair memories rise up before me like the forms of departed gods.... They come, not thronging in crowds, in slow procession they follow one another like those draped Athenian figures we admired so much—dost thou remember?—in the ancient bas-reliefs in the Vatican.

VI

I have spoken of the light that comes from the heart of man, and sheds brightness on all around him... I long to talk with thee of the time when in my heart too that light burned bright with blessing... Listen... and I will fancy sitting before me, gazing up at me with those eyes—so fond yet stern almost in their intentness. O eyes, never to be forgotten! On whom are they fastened now? Who folds in his heart thy glance—that glance that seems to flow from depths unknown even as mysterious springs—like ye, both clear and dark—that gush out into some narrow, deep ravine under the frowning cliffs.... Listen.

VII

It was at the end of March before Annunciation, soon after I had seen thee for the first time and—not yet dreaming of what thou wouldst be to me—already, silently, secretly, I bore thee in my heart. I chanced to cross one of the great rivers of Russia. The ice had not yet broken up but looked swollen and dark; it was the fourth day of thaw. The snow was melting everywhere—steadily but slowly; there was the running of water on all sides; a noiseless wind strayed in the soft air. Earth and sky alike were steeped in one unvarying milky hue; there was not fog nor was there light; not one object stood out clear in the general whiteness, everything looked both close and indistinct. I left my cart far behind and walked swiftly over the ice of the river, and except the muffled thud of my own steps heard not a sound. I went on enfolded on all sides by the first breath, the first thrill of early spring... and gradually gaining force with every step, with every movement forwards, a glad tremour sprang up and grew, all uncomprehended within me... it drew me on, it hastened me, and so strong was the flood of gladness within me, that I stood still at last and with questioning eyes looked round me, as I would seek some outer cause of my mood of rapture.... All was soft, white, slumbering, but I lifted my eyes; high in the heavens floated a flock of birds flying back to us.... 'Spring! welcome spring!' I shouted aloud: 'welcome, life and love and happiness!' And at that instance, with sweetly troubling shock, suddenly like a cactus flower thy image blossomed aflame within me, blossomed and grew, bewilderingly fair and radiant, and I knew that I love thee, thee only—that I am all filled full of thee....

VIII

I think of thee... and many other memories, other pictures float before me with thee everywhere, at every turn of my life I meet thee. Now an old Russian garden rises up before me on the slope of a hillside, lighted up by the last rays of the summer sun. Behind the silver poplars peeps out the wooden roof of the manor-house with a thin curl of reddish smoke above the white chimney, and in the fence a little gate stands just ajar, as though some one had drawn it to with faltering hand; and I stand and wait and gaze at that gate and the sand of the garden path—wonder and rapture in my heart. All that I behold seems new and different; over all a breath of some glad, brooding mystery, and already I catch the swift rustle of steps, and I stand intent and alert as a bird with wings folded ready to take flight anew, and my heart burns and shudders in joyous dread before the approaching, the alighting rapture....

IX

Then I see an ancient cathedral in a beautiful, far-off land. In rows kneel the close packed people; a breath of prayerful chill, of something grave and melancholy is wafted from the high, bare roof, from the huge, branching columns. Thou standest at my side, mute, apart, as though knowing me not. Each fold of thy dark cloak hangs motionless as carved in stone. Motionless, too, lie the bright patches cast by the stained windows at thy feet on the worn flags. And lo, violently thrilling the incense-clouded air, thrilling us within, rolled out the mighty flood of the organ's notes... and I saw thee paler, rigid—thy glance caressed me, glided higher and rose heavenwards—while to me it seemed none but an immortal soul could look so, with such eyes...

X

Another picture comes back to me.

No old-world temple subdues us with its stern magnificence; the low walls of a little snug room shut us off from the whole world. What am I saying? We are alone, alone in the whole world; except us two there is nothing living—outside these friendly walls darkness and death and emptiness... It is not the wind that howls without, not the rain streaming in floods; without, Chaos wails and moans, his sightless eyes are weeping. But with us all is peaceful and light and warm and welcoming; something droll, something of childish innocence, like a butterfly—isn't it so?—flutters about us. We nestle close to one another; we lean our heads together and both read a favourite book. I feel the delicate vein beating in thy soft forehead; I hear that thou livest, thou hearest that I am living, thy smile is born on my face before it is on thine, thou makest mute answer to my mute question, thy thoughts, my thoughts are like the two wings of one bird, lost in the infinite blue... the last barriers have fallen—and so soothed, so deepened is our love, so utterly has all apartness vanished that we have no need for word or look to pass between us.... Only to breathe, to breathe together is all we want, to be together and scarcely to be conscious that we are together....

XI

Or last of all, there comes before me that bright September when we walked through the deserted, still flowering garden of a forsaken palace on the bank of a great river—not Russian—under the soft brilliance of the cloudless sky. Oh, how put into words what we felt! The endlessly flowing river, the solitude and peace and bliss, and a kind of voluptuous melancholy, and the thrill of rapture, the unfamiliar monotonous town, the autumn cries of the jackdaws in the high sun-lit treetops, and the tender words and smiles and looks, long, soft, piercing to the very in-most soul, and the beauty, beauty in our lives, about us, on all sides—it is above words. Oh, the bench on which we sat in silence with heads bowed down under the weight of feeling—I cannot forget it till the hour I die! How delicious were those few strangers passing us with brief greetings and kind faces, and the great quiet boats floating by (in one—dost thou remember?—stood a horse pensively gazing at the gliding water), the baby prattle of the tiny ripples by the bank, and the very bark of the distant dogs across the water, the very shouts of the fat officer drilling the red-faced recruits yonder, with outspread arms and knees crooked like grasshoppers!... We both felt that better than those moments nothing in the world had been or would be for us, that all else... But why compare? Enough... enough... Alas! yes: enough.

XII

For the last time I give myself up to those memories and bid them farewell forever. So, a miser gloating over his hoard, his gold, his bright treasure, covers it over in the damp, grey earth; so; the wick of a smouldering lamp flickers up in a last bright flare and sinks into cold ash. The wild creature has peeped out from its hole for the last time at the velvet grass, the sweet sun, the blue, kindly waters, and has huddled back into the depths, curled up, and gone to sleep. Will he have glimpses even in the sleep of the sweet sun and the grass and the blue kindly water?...

XIII

Sternly, remorselessly, fate leads each of us, and only at the first, absorbed in details of all sorts, in trifles, in ourselves, we are not aware of her harsh hand. While one can be deceived and has no shame in lying, one can live and there is no shame in hoping. Truth, not the full truth, of that, indeed, we cannot speak, but even that little we can reach locks up our lips at once, ties our hands, leads us to 'the No.' Then one way is left a man to keep his feet, not to fall to pieces, not to sink into the mire of self-forgetfulness... of self-contempt,—calmly to turn away from all, to say 'enough!' and folding impotent arms upon the empty breast, to save the last, the sole honour he can attain to, the dignity of knowing his own nothingness; that dignity at which Pascal hints when calling man a thinking reed he says that if the whole universe crushed him, he, that reed, would be higher than the universe, because he would know it was crushing him, and it would know it not. A poor dignity! A sorry consolation! Try your utmost to be penetrated by it, to have faith in it, you, whoever you may be, my poor brother, and there's no refuting those words of menace:

'Life's but a walking shadow, a poor player,

That struts and frets his hour upon the stage
And then it is heard no more: it is a tale
Told by an idiot, full of sound and fury
Signifying nothing.'

I quoted these lines from *Macbeth*, and there came back to my mind the witches, phantoms, apparitions.... Alas! no ghosts, no fantastic, unearthly powers are terrible; there are no terrors in the Hoffmann world, in whatever form it appears.... What is terrible is that there is nothing terrible, that the very essence of life is petty, uninteresting and degradingly inane. Once one is soaked through and through with that knowledge, once one has tasted of that bitter, no honey more seems sweet, and even the highest, sweetest bliss, the bliss of love, of perfect nearness, of complete devotion—even that loses all its magic; all its dignity is destroyed by its own pettiness, its brevity. Yes, a man loved, glowed with passion, murmured of eternal bliss, of undying raptures, and lo, no trace is left of the very worm that devoured the last relic of his withered tongue. So, on a frosty day in late autumn, when all is lifeless and dumb in the bleached grey grass, on the bare forest edge, if the sun but come out for an instant from the fog and turn one steady glance on the frozen earth, at once the gnats swarm up on all sides; they sport in the warm rays, bustle, flutter up and down, circle round one another... The sun is hidden—the gnats fall in a feeble shower, and there is the end of their momentary life.

XIV

But are there no great conceptions, no great words of consolation: patriotism, right, freedom, humanity, art? Yes, those words there are, and many men live by them and for them. And yet it seems to me that if Shakespeare could be born again he would have no cause to retract his Hamlet, his Lear. His searching glance would discover nothing new in human life: still the same motley picture—in reality so little complex—would unroll before him in its terrifying sameness. The same credulity and the same cruelty, the same lust of blood, of gold, of filth, the same vulgar pleasures, the same senseless sufferings in the name... why, in the name of the very same shams that Aristophanes jeered at two thousand years ago, the same coarse snares in which the many-headed beast, the multitude, is caught so easily, the same workings of power, the same traditions of slavishness, the same innateness of falsehood—in a word, the same busy squirrel's turning in the same old unchanged wheel.... Again, Shakespeare would set Lear repeating his cruelty: 'None doth offend,' which in other words means: 'None is without offence.' and he too would say 'enough!' he too would turn away. One thing perhaps, may be: in contrast to the gloomy tragic tyrant Richard, the great poet's ironic genius who would want to paint a newer type, the tyrant of today, who is almost ready to believe in his own virtue, and sleeps well of nights, or finds fault with too sumptuous a dinner at the very time when his half-crushed victims try to find comfort in picturing him, like Richard, haunted by the phantoms of those he has ruined...

But to what end?

Why prove—picking out, too, and weighing words, smoothing and rounding off phrases—why prove to gnats that they are really gnats?

XV

But art?... beauty?... Yes, these are words of power; they are more powerful, maybe, than those I have spoken before. The Venus of Milo is, maybe, more real than Roman law or the principles of 1789. It may be objected—how many times has the retort been heard!—that beauty itself is relative; that by the Chinese it is conceived as quite other than the European's ideal.... But it is not the relativity of art confounds me; its transitoriness, again its brevity, its dust and ashes—that is what robs me of faith and courage. Art at a given moment is more powerful, may be, than nature; for in nature is no symphony of Beethoven, no picture of Ruysdäel, no poem of Goethe, and only dull-witted pedants or disingenuous chatterers can yet maintain that art is the imitation of nature. But at the end of all, nature is inexorable; she has no need to hurry, and sooner or later she takes her own. Unconsciously and inflexibly obedient to laws, she knows not art, as she knows not freedom, as she knows not good; from all ages moving, from all ages changing, she suffers nothing immortal, nothing unchanging.... Man is her child; but man's work—art—is hostile to her, just because it strives to be unchanging and immortal. Man is the child of nature; but she is the universal mother, and she has no preferences; all that exists in her lap has arisen only at the cost of something else and must in its time yield its place to something else. She creates destroying, and she cares not whether she creates, or she destroys—so long as life be not exterminated, so long as death fall not short of his dues.... And so just as serenely she hides in mould the god-like shape of Phidias's Zeus as the simplest pebble and gives the vile worm for food the priceless verse of Sophokles. Mankind, 'tis true, jealously aid her in her work of...of slaughter; but is it not the same elemental force, the force of nature, that finds vent in the fist of the barbarian recklessly smashing the radiant brow of Apollo, in the savage yells with which he casts in the fire the picture of Apelles? How are we, poor folks, poor artists to be a match for this deaf, dumb, blind force who triumphs not even in her conquests, but goes onward, onward, devouring all things? How stand against those coarse and mighty waves, endlessly, unceasingly moving upward? How have faith in the value and dignity of the fleeting images, that in the dark, on the edge of the abyss, we shape out of dust for an instant?

XVI

All this is true,... but only the transient is beautiful, said Schiller; and nature in the incessant play of her rising, vanishing forms is not averse to beauty. Does not she carefully deck the most fleeting of her children—the petals of the flowers, the wings of the butterfly—in the fairest hues, does she not give them the most exquisite lines? Beauty needs not to live forever to be eternal—one instant is enough for her. Yes, that may be is true—but only there where personality is not, where man is not, where freedom is not; the butterfly's wing spoiled appears again and again for a thousand years as the same wing of the same butterfly; there sternly, fairly, impersonally necessity completes her circle... but man is not repeated like the butterfly, and the work of his hands, his art, his spontaneous creation once destroyed is lost forever.... To him alone is it vouchsafed to create... but strange and dreadful it is to pronounce: we are creators... for one hour—as there was, in the tale, a caliph for an hour. In this is our pre-eminence—and our curse; each of those 'creators' himself, even he and no other, even this *I* is, as it were, constructed with certain aim, on lines laid down beforehand; each more or less dimly is aware of his significance, is aware that he is innately something noble, eternal—and lives, and must live in the moment and for the moment.[1] Sit in the mud, my friend, and aspire to the skies! The greatest among us are just those who more deeply than all others have felt this rooted contradiction; though if so, it may be asked, can such words be used as greatest, great?

[Footnote 1: One cannot help recalling here Mephistopheles's words to Faust:—

'Er (Gott) findet sich in einem ewgen Glanze,

Uns hat er in die Finsterniss gebracht—

Und euch taugt einzig Tag und Nacht.'

—AUTHOR'S NOTE.]

XVII

What is to be said of those to whom, with all goodwill, one cannot apply such terms, even in the sense given them by the feeble tongue of man? What can one say of the ordinary, common, second-rate, third-rate toilers—whatsoever they may be—statesmen, men of science, artists—above all, artists? How conjure them to shake off their numb indolence, their weary stupor, how draw them back to the field of battle, if once the conception has stolen into their brains of the nullity of everything human, of every sort of effort that sets before itself a higher aim than the mere winning of bread? By what crowns can they be lured for whom laurels and thorns alike are valueless? For what end will they again face the laughter of 'the unfeeling crowd' or 'the judgment of the fool'—of the old fool who cannot forgive them from turning away from the old bogies—of the young fool who would force them to kneel with him, to grovel with him before the new, lately discovered idols? Why should they go back again into that jostling crowd of phantoms, to that market-place where seller and buyer cheat each other alike, where there is noise and clamour, and all is paltry and worthless? Why 'with impotence in their bones' should they struggle back into that world where the peoples, like peasant boys on a holiday, are tussling in the mire for handfuls of empty nutshells, or gape in open-mouthed adoration before sorry tinsel-decked pictures, into that world where only that is living which has no right to live, and each, stifling self with his own shouting, hurries feverishly to an unknown, uncomprehended goal? No... no.... Enough... enough... enough!

XVIII

The rest is silence. [Footnote: English in the original.—TRANSLATOR'S NOTE.]

1864.

END